TERROR IN AN UNKNOWN WORLD

... we saw a horrible sight once at the colliery pits, where a slave worker had the misfortune to cut his hand. In an instant, coming from all quarters, thousands of red fish not much longer than a herring, with large mouths and formidable rows of teeth, were on to him. The lower part of him, beneath his bell, dissolved before our eyes amid the cloud of vibrant life which surrounded him. One instant we saw a man. The next there was a red mass with white protruding bones. A minute later the bones only were left below the waist and half a clean-picked skeleton was lying at the bottom of the sea ...

THE MARACOT DEEP

by

Sir Arthur Conan Doyle

With an Introduction by
John Dickson Carr

Published by
MODERN PROMOTIONS
A Division of Unisystems Inc.
New York, N.Y.

INTRODUCTION

Everybody knows Sir Arthur Conan Doyle as the creator of Sherlock Holmes. Discriminating readers will also name him as author of some of the finest historical romances in the language. Whether he set his characters at high adventure amid the chivalric uproar of the fourteenth century, as with *The White Company* and *Sir Nigel*, or in black Canadian forests echoing to the war-whoop of the Iroquois, as with *The Refugees*, or against the roaring days of Napoleonic Europe, as with the many adventures of Brigadier Gerard, his touch was as sure as his background was accurate. And not the least achievement of this many-sided man—doctor, historian, criminologist, war correspondent as well as boxer, cricketer, and ski enthusiast—lay in the field of what nowadays we know as science fiction.

Who first called it "science fiction"?

Perhaps some philologist or lexicographer can supply the answer at once; I regret to say I can't. The term had not been invented when Edgar Allan Poe wrote "The Balloon Hoax," "A Descent into the Maelstrom," and "The Unparalleled Adventure of One Hans Pfall." It was unknown to Jules Verne, whose life-span (1828–1905) saw the development of so many wonders he had forecast in fantasy; the submarine saga of *Twenty Thousand Leagues Under the Sea* appeared as early as 1870. When toward the end of the nineteenth century H. G. Wells weighed in with his own startling prophecies, some of which have not been realized even yet, it was still loosely called the scientific romance.

"Science fiction," as a term at least, seems to have sprung up almost by itself; like Topsy, it just growed. We need not quibble about semantics. The Americans, the French, the British were pioneers in the field; they dominate it to this day. It has not always been easy going. We must remember the plight of the poor-devil writer who dreamed up an atom bomb at a time when the backroom boys were actually constructing one, and saw endless trouble before he could persuade anybody to believe in his innocence. But the pioneers of the field all enjoyed themselves hugely, and none of them enjoyed himself more than did Sir Arthur Conan Doyle.

When he was still plain Dr. Conan Doyle, a struggling young physician at Portsmouth on the south coast of England, he wrote his first venture in science fiction for the *Cornhill Magazine* during the early 1880's. A short story called "Habakkuk Jephson's Statement," it dealt with what still remains one of the great sea mysteries: the problem of the derelict ship *Mary Celeste*, found drifting with not a soul aboard and few clues as to what fate could have overtaken her crew.

Well, that first venture provoked a first-class row.

No small part of our author's genius was his ability

to tell a story so persuasively that it sounded like a narration of fact. "Habakkuk Jephson's Statement," though written as fiction and presented as such by the magazine, fell into the hands of a certain British official named Solly Flood, Her Majesty's Advocate-General at Gibraltar, who took it as a pretended eyewitness account of the whole affair.

Whereupon Mr. Flood wrote to the newspapers, indignantly denouncing Habakkuk Jephson as an impostor who didn't know the facts. It was all a damn lie, Mr. Flood said in effect, and he could prove it was a lie. What did Habakkuk Jephson have to say *now*?"

Though the spectacle of officialdom making an ass of itself is always wholly satisfying, it may be doubted that Mr. Flood to the end of his life ever saw the joke.

Several times in later years Conan Doyle returned to the short story of science fiction. One such tale, if this can be credited, is a comedy of the electric chair at a time when electricity constituted a new means of execution. A mining town in the American Old West, determined on being progressive, sets up an electric chair as a deterrent to evildoers.

But when they try it out on a notorious bad man who deserves death ten times over ("Touch her off!" roars the desperado, sitting down), something goes wrong. They jolt the victim with too much electricity; far from killing him according to plan, they succeed only in curing his rheumatism and making him all but deathless. The execution, to the joy of all humane people, must be indefinitely postponed; and so ends "The Los Amigos Fiasco."

With "The Horror of the Heights," a grim and grisly affair, Conan Doyle envisaged perils which might lurk in the upper air; and, though today we travel such sky lanes without a tremor of fear, the author's extrapolation was valid at the time he wrote it. In "Danger!" he warned of the German submarine menace before this menace became a terrible reality during World War I.

But it was with his novels, and with a set of characters as engaging as Dumas's musketeers, that he took his rightful place in the hierarchy of the scientific romance.

He was past fifty—knighted, well-to-do, and full of honors—when he encountered Professor Ray Lankester's book on extinct animals, those monsters of tooth and claw which roamed the earth's surface in the morning of creation. Suppose, say on some highplateau in the jungles of the Amazon, such monsters still existed? What quarry for a big-game hunter! What wonders for a zoologist! And in 1912 appeared what some consider his masterpiece, *The Lost World*.

If up to this time any complaint had been uttered against the scientific romance, it was that such stories sometimes contained too much science and too little romance. It is a complaint not infrequently heard today, when we have grown almost too sophisticated. The science must be right; the science *is* right, even when it squeezes the story dry of humor and humanity alike. But to exclude humor or humanity from any kind of chronicle was a mistake never made by Arthur Conan Doyle.

As his inspiration for Sherlock Holmes had been one of his professors at Edinburgh University—Joseph Bell, the surgeon—so as his model for the protagonist of *The Lost World* he chose another Edinburgh teacher—Professor Rutherford, the zoologist, a stunted Hercules with a booming voice and a black beard like an Assyrian bull. Through this tale of high adventure in South America romps and roars Professor George Edward Challenger: at once brilliant, violent, childish, outrageous, and funny. Beside him stalk the other three musketeers: acid-tongued Professor Summerlee; the millionaire sportsman, Lord

John Roxton; and the eternally sympathetic Irish newspaperman, Edward Malone of the *Daily Gazette*.

A year later the same group of characters returned in *The Poison Belt*, to meet events just as dangerous though they took place no farther from home than Conan Doyle's own county of Sussex. Professor Challenger subsequently reappears in one science-fiction novelette and one science-fiction short story, in the latter of which he threatens an injunction against the telephone company for letting his phone ring when he wants to be undisturbed. Nor is the reason for Challenger's vitality far to seek.

His creator was really fond of Challenger, the explosive one; he enjoyed Challenger more than any character he had ever created. He would imitate Challenger for the edification of family and friends. He had himself photographed as Challenger, decked out with false beard and adhesive eyebrows. In his Challenger get-up, acting to the top of his bent, he once called on his brother-in-law, Willie Hornung, and precipitated family trouble when Willie penetrated his disguise.

Sitting down to write *The Maracot Deep*, the short science-fiction novel which follows, Conan Doyle was well past his sixtieth year. No longer could George Edward Challenger figure as protagonist. In *The Land of Mist*, a fundamentally serious novel published only a few years before, he had used the turbulent zoologist to express his own philosophy of life. But, if new characters were needed, the old master could meet that challenge too. And so we have Professor Maracot, Cyrus Headley, and Bill Scanlan, with their exploits below the bottom of the sea.

Maracot, let it be confessed, is not Challenger. The American slang of the 1920's sometimes rings strangely on the ear. But here is high adventure of the true vintage; here is scarifying danger as well as disaster turned to triumph; the means used to communicate without words, a forerunner of today's television, shows triumphant ingenuity. As Conan Doyle's biographer I enjoyed it immensely, and I think you will enjoy it too.

JOHN DICKSON CARR

THE MARACOT DEEP

CHAPTER I

Since these papers have been put into my hands to edit, I will begin by reminding the public of the sad loss of the steamship *Stratford*, which started a year ago upon a voyage for the purpose of oceanography and the study of deep-sea life. The expedition had been organized by Dr. Maracot, the famous author of *Pseudo-Coralline Formations* and *The Morphology of the Lamellibrachs*. Dr. Maracot had with him Mr. Cyrus Headley, formerly assistant at the Zoological Institute of Cambridge, Massachusetts, and at the time of the voyage Rhodes Scholar at Oxford. Captain Howie, an experienced navigator, was in charge of the vessel, and there was a crew of twenty-three men, including an American mechanic from the Merribank Works, Philadelphia.

This whole party has utterly disappeared, and the only word ever heard of the ill-fated steamer was from the report of a Norwegian barque which actually saw a ship, closely corresponding with her description, go down in the great gale of the autumn of 1926. A lifeboat marked *Stratford* was found later in the neighbourhood of the tragedy, together with some deck gratings, a lifebuoy, and a spar. This, coupled with the long silence, seemed to make it absolutely sure that the vessel and her crew would never be heard of more. Her fate is rendered more certain by the strange wireless message received at the time, which, though incomprehensible in parts, left little doubt as to the fate of the vessel. This I will quote later.

There were some remarkable points about the voyage of the *Stratford* which caused comment at the time. One was the curious secrecy observed by Professor Maracot. He was famous for his dislike and distrust of the press, but it was pushed to an extreme upon this occasion, when he would neither give information to reporters nor would he permit the representative of any paper to set foot in the vessel during the weeks that it lay in the Albert Dock. There were rumours abroad of some curious and novel construction of the ship which would fit it for deep-sea work, and these rumours were confirmed from the yard of Hunter and Company of West Hartlepool, where the structural changes had actually been carried out. It was at one time said that the whole bottom of the vessel was detachable, a report which attracted the attention of the underwriters at Lloyd's, who were, with some difficulty, satisfied upon the point. The matter was soon forgotten, but it assumes an importance now when the fate of the expedition has been brought once more in so extraordinary a manner to the notice of the public.

So much for the beginning of the voyage of the *Stratford*. There are now four documents which cover the facts so far as they are known. The first is the letter which was written by Mr. Cyrus Headley, from the capital of the Grand Canary, to his friend, Sir James Talbot, of Trinity College, Oxford, upon the only occasion, so far as is known, when the *Stratford* touched land after leaving the Thames. The second is the strange wireless call to which I have alluded. The third is that portion of the log of the *Arabella Knowles* which deals with the vitreous ball. The fourth and last is the amazing contents of that receptacle, which either represent a most cruel and complex mystification, or else open up a fresh chapter in human experience the importance of which cannot be exaggerated. With this preamble, I will now give Mr. Headley's letter, which I owe to the courtesy of Sir James Talbot, and which has not previously been published. It is dated October 1, 1926.

I am mailing this, my dear Talbot, from Porta de la Luz, where we have put in for a few days of rest. My principal companion in the voyage has been Bill Scanlan, the head mechanic, who, as a fellow-countryman and also as a very entertaining character, has become my natural associate. However, I am alone this morning as he has what he describes as "a date with a skirt." You see, he talks as Englishmen expect every real American to talk. He would be accepted as the true breed. The mere force of suggestion makes me "guess" and "reckon" when I am with my English friends. I feel that they would never really understand that I was a Yankee if I did not. However, I am not on those terms with you, so let me assure you right now that you will not find anything but pure Oxford in the epistle which I am now mailing to you.

You met Maracot at the Mitre, so you know the dry chip of a man that he is. I told you, I think, how he came to pitch upon me for the job. He inquired from old Somerville of the Zoological Institute, who sent him my prize essay on the pelagic crabs, and that did the trick. Of course, it is splendid to be on such a congenial errand, but I wish it wasn't with such an animated mummy as Maracot. He is inhuman in his isolation and his devotion to his work. "The world's stiffest stiff," says Bill Scanlan. And yet you can't but admire such complete devotion. Nothing exists outside his own science. I remember that you laughed when I asked him what I ought to read as a preparation, and he said that for serious study I should read the collected edition of his own works, but for relaxation Haeckel's *Plankton-Studien*.

I know him no better now than I did in that little parlour looking out on the Oxford High. He says nothing, and his gaunt, austere face—the face of a Savonarola, or rather, perhaps, of a Torquemada—never relapses into geniality. The long, thin, aggressive nose, the two small gleaming gray eyes set closely together under a thatch of eyebrows, the thin-lipped, compressed mouth, the cheeks worn into hollows by constant thought and ascetic life, are all uncompanionable. He lives on some mental mountaintop, out of reach of ordinary mortals. Sometimes I think he is a little mad. For example, this extraordinary instrument that he has made . . . but I'll tell things in their due order and then you can judge for yourself.

I'll take our voyage from the start. The *Stratford* is a fine seaworthy little boat, specially fitted for her job. She is twelve hundred tons, with clear decks and a good broad beam, furnished with every possible appliance for sounding, trawling, dredging, and tow-netting. She has, of course, powerful steam winches for hauling in the trawls, and a number of other gadgets of various kinds, some of which are familiar enough, and some are strange. Below these are comfortable quarters with a well-fitted laboratory for our special studies.

We had the reputation of being a mystery ship before we started, and I soon found that it was not undeserved. Our first proceedings were commonplace enough. We took a turn up the North Sea and dropped our trawls for a scrape or two, but, as the average depth is not much over sixty feet and we were specially fitted for very deep-sea work, it seemed rather a waste of time. Anyhow, save for familiar table fish, dog-fish, squids, jellyfish, and some terrigenous bottom deposits of the usual alluvial clay-mud, we got nothing worth writing home about. Then we rounded Scotland, sighted the Faroes, and came down the Wyville-Thomson Ridge, where we had better luck. Thence we worked south to our proper cruising-ground, which was between the African coast and these islands. We nearly grounded on Fuert-Eventura one moonless night, but save for that our voyage was uneventful.

During these first weeks I tried to make friends with Maracot, but it was not easy work. First of all, he is the most absorbed and absent-minded man in the world. You will remember how you smiled when he gave the elevator boy a penny under the impression that he was in a street car. Half the time he is utterly lost in his thoughts, and seems hardly aware of where he is or what he is doing. Then in the second place he is secretive to the last degree. He is continually working at papers and charts, which he shuffles away when I happen to enter the cabin. It is my firm belief that the man has some secret project in his mind, but that so long as we are due to touch at any port he will keep it to himself. That is the impression which I have received, and I find that Bill Scanlan is of the same opinion.

"Say, Mr. Headley," said he one evening, when I was seated in the laboratory testing out the salinity of samples from our hydrographic soundings, "what d'you figure out that this guy has in his mind? What d'you reckon that he means to do?"

"I suppose," said I, "that we shall do what the *Challenger* and a dozen other exploring ships have done before us, and add a few more species to the list of fish and a few more entries to the bathymetric chart."

"Not on your life," said he. "If that's your opinion you've got to guess again. First of all, what am I here for, anyhow?"

"In case the machinery goes wrong," I hazarded.

"Machinery nothing! The ship's machinery is in charge of MacLaren, the Scotch engineer. No, sir, it wasn't to run a donkey-engine that the Merribank folk sent out their star performer. If I pull down fifty bucks a week it's not for nix. Come here, and I'll make you wise to it."

He took a key from his pocket and opened a door at the back of the laboratory which led us down a companion ladder to a section of the hold which was cleared right across save for four large glittering objects half-exposed amid the straw of their huge packing-cases. They were flat sheets of steel with elaborate bolts and rivets along the edges. Each sheet was about ten foot square and an inch and a half thick, with a circular gap of eighteen inches in the middle.

"What in thunder is it?" I asked.

Bill Scanlan's face—he looks halfway between a vaudeville comic and a prize-fighter—broke into a grin at my astonishment.

"That's my baby, sir," he quoted. "Yes. Mr. Headley, that's what I am here for. There is a steel bottom to the thing. It's in that big case yonder. Then there is a top, kind of arched, and a great ring for a chain or rope. Now, look here at the bottom of the ship."

There was a square wooden platform there, with projecting screws at each corner which showed that it was detachable.

"There is a double bottom," said Scanlan. "It may be that this guy is clean loco, or it may be that he has more in his block than we know, but if I read him right he means to build up a kind of room—the windows are in storage here—and lower it through the bottom of the ship. He's got electric searchlights here, and I allow that he plans to shine 'em through the round portholes and see what's goin' on around."

"He could have put a crystal sheet into the ship, like the Cataline Island boats, if that was all that was in his mind," said I.

"You've said a mouthful," said Bill Scanlan, scratching his head. "I can't figger it out nohow. The only one sure thing is, that I've been sent to be under his orders and to help him with the darn fool thing all I can. He has said nothin' up to now, so I've said the same, but I'll just snoop around, and if I wait long enough I'll learn all there is to know."

So that was how I first got on to the edge of our mystery. We ran into some dirty weather after that, and then we got to work doing some deep-sea trawling northwest of Cape Juba, just outside the Continental Slope, and taking temperature readings and salinity records. It's a sporting proposition, this deep-sea dragging with a Peterson otter trawl gaping twenty feet wide for everything that comes its way—sometimes down a quarter of a mile and bringing up one lot of fish, sometimes half a mile and quite a different lot, every stratum of ocean with its own inhabitants as separate as so many continents. Sometimes from the bottom we would just bring up half a ton of clear pink jelly, the raw material of life, or, maybe, it would be a scoop of pteropod ooze, breaking up under the microscope into millions of tiny round reticulated balls with amorphous mud between. I won't bore you with all the brotulids and macrurids, the ascidians and holothurians, and polyzoa and echinoderms—anyhow, you can reckon that there is a great harvest in the sea, and that we have been dilligent reapers. But always I had the same feeling that the heart of Maracot was not in the job, and that other plans were in that queer, high, narrow Egyptian mummy of a head.

It all seemed to me to be a try-out of men and things until the real business got going.

I had got as far as this in my letter when I went ashore to have a last stretch, for we sail in the early morning. It's as well, perhaps, that I did go, for there was no end of a barney going on upon the pier, with Maracot and Bill Scanlan right in the heart of it. Bill is a bit of a scrapper, and has what he calls a mean wallop in both mitts, but with half-a-dozen Dagoes with knives all round them things looked ugly, and it was time that I butted in. It seems that the Doctor had hired one of the things they call cabs, and had driven half over the island inspecting the geology, but had clean forgotten that he had no money on him. When it came to paying, he could not make these country hicks understand, and the cabman had grabbed his watch so as to make sure. That brought Bill Scanlan into action, and they would have both been on the floor with their backs like pincushions if I had not squared the matter up, with a dollar or two over for the driver and a five-dollar bonus for the chap with the mouse under his eye. So all ended well, and Maracot was more human than ever I saw him yet. When we got to the ship he called me into the little cabin which he reserves for himself and he thanked me.

"By the way, Mr. Headley," he said, "I understand that you are not a married man?"

"No," said I, "I am not."

"No one depending upon you?"

"No."

"Good!" said he. "I have not spoken of the object of this voyage because I have, for my own reasons, desired it to be secret. One of those reasons was that I feared to be forestalled. When scientific plans get about one may be served as Scott was served by Amundsen. Had Scott kept his counsel as I have done, it would be he and not Amundsen who would have been the first at the South Pole. For my part, I have quite as important a destination as the South Pole, and so I have been silent. But now we are on the eve of our great adventure and no rival has time to steal my plans. To-morrow we start for our real goal."

"And what is that?" I asked.

He leaned forward, his ascetic face all lit up with the enthusiasm of the fanatic.

"Our goal," said he, "is the bottom of the Atlantic Ocean."

And right here I ought to stop, for I expect it has taken away your breath as it did mine. If I were a story-writer, I guess I should leave it at that. But as I am just a chronicler of what occurred, I may tell you that I stayed another hour in the cabin of old man Maracot, and that I learned a lot, which there is still just time for me to tell you before the last shore boat leaves.

"Yes, young man," said he, "you may write freely now, for by the time your letter reaches England we shall have made the plunge."

This started him sniggering, for he has a queer dry sense of humour of his own.

"Yes, sir, the plunge is the right word on this occasion, a plunge which will be historic in the annals of Science. Let me tell you, in the first place, that I am well convinced that the current doctrine as to the extreme pressure of the ocean at great depths is entirely misleading. It is perfectly clear that other factors exist which neutralize the effect, though I am not yet prepared to say what those factors may be. That is one of the problems which we may settle. Now, what pressure, may I ask, have you been led to expect under a mile of water?" He glowered at me through his big horn spectacles.

"Not less than a ton to the square inch," I answered. "Surely that has been clearly shown."

"The task of the pioneer has always been to disprove the thing which has been clearly shown. Use your brains, young man. You have been for the last month fishing up some of the most delicate bathic forms of life, creatures so delicate that you could hardly transfer them from the net to the tank without marring their sensitive shapes. Did you find that there was evidence upon them of this extreme pressure?"

"The pressure," said I, "equalized itself. It was the same within as without."

"Words—mere words!" he cried, shaking his lean head impatiently. "You have brought up round fish, such fish as Gastrostomus globulus. Would they not have been squeezed flat had the pressure been as you imagine? Or look at our otter-boards. They are not squeezed together at the mouth of the trawl."

"But the experience of divers?"

"Certainly it holds good up to a point. They do find a sufficient increase of pressure to influence what is perhaps the most sensitive organ of the body, the interior of the ear. But as I plan it, we shall not be exposed to any pressure at all. We shall be lowered in a steel cage with crystal windows on each side for observation. If the pressure is not strong enough to break in an inch and a half of toughened double-nickelled steel, then it cannot hurt us. It is an extension of the experiment of the Williamson Brothers at Nassau, with which no doubt you are familiar. If my calculation is wrong—well, you say that no one is dependent upon you. We shall die in a great adventure. Of course, if you would rather stand clear, I can go alone."

It seemed to me the maddest kind of scheme, and yet you know how difficult it is to refuse a dare. I played for time while I thought it over.

"How deep do you propose to go, sir?" I asked.

He had a chart pinned upon the table, and he placed the end of his compasses upon a point which lies to the southwest of the Canaries.

"Last year I did some sounding in this part," said he. "There is a pit of great depth. We got twenty-five thousand feet there. I was the first to report it. Indeed, I trust that you will find it on the charts of the future as the 'Maracot Deep.'"

"But, good God, sir!" I cried, "you don't propose to descend into an abyss like that?"

"No, no," he answered, smiling. "Neither our lowering chain nor our air tubes reach beyond half a mile. But I was going to explain to you that round this deep crevasse, which has no doubt been formed by volcanic forces long ago, there is a raised ridge or narrow plateau, which is not more than three hundred fathoms under the surface."

"Three hundred fathoms! A third of a mile!"

"Yes, roughly a third of a mile. It is my present intention that we shall be lowered in our little pressure-proof look-out station on to this submarine bank. There we shall make such observations as we can. A speaking-tube will connect us with the ship so that we can give our directions. There should be no difficulty in the matter. When we wish to be hauled up we have only to say so."

"And the air?"

"Will be pumped down to us."

"But it will be pitch-dark."

"That, I fear, is undoubtedly true. The experiments of Fol and Sarasin at the Lake of Geneva show that even the ultra-violet rays are absent at that depth. But does it matter? We shall be provided with the powerful electric illumination from the ship's engines, supplemented by six two-volt Hellesens dry cells connected together so as to give a current of twelve volts.

That, with a Lucas army signalling lamp as a movable reflector, should serve our turn. Any other difficulties?"

"If our air lines tangle?"

"They won't tangle. And as a reserve we have compressed air in tubes which would last us twenty-four hours. Well, have I satisfied you? Will you come?"

It was not an easy decision. The brain works quickly and imagination is a mighty vivid thing. I seemed to realize that black box down in the primeval depths, to feel the foul twice-breathed air, and then to see the walls sagging, bulging inwards, rending at the joints with the water spouting in at every rivet-hole and crevice and crawling up from below. It was a slow, dreadful death to die. But I looked up, and there were the old man's fiery eyes fixed upon me with the exaltation of a martyr to Science. It's catching, that sort of enthusiasm, and if it be crazy, it is at least noble and unselfish. I caught fire from his great flame, and I sprang to my feet with my hand out.

"Doctor, I'm with you to the end," said I.

"I knew it," said he. "It was not for your smattering of learning that I picked you, my young friend, nor," he added, smiling, "for your intimate acquaintance with the pelagic crabs. There are other qualities which may be more immediately useful, and they are loyalty and courage."

So with that little bit of sugar I was dismissed, with my future pledged and my whole scheme of life in ruins. Well, the last shore boat is leaving. They are calling for the mail. You will either not hear from me again, my dear Talbot, or you will get a letter worth reading. If you don't hear you can have a floating headstone and drop it somewhere south of the Canaries with the inscription: "Here, or Hereabouts, lies all that the fishes have left of my friend.

"CYRUS J. HEADLEY."

The second document in the case is the unintelligible wireless message which was intercepted by several vessels, including the Royal Mail steamer *Arroya*. It was received at 3 PM, October 3, 1926, which shows that it was dispatched only two days after the *Stratford* left the Grand Canary, as shown in the previous letter, and it corresponds roughly with the time when the Norwegian barque saw a steamer founder in a cyclone two hundred miles to the southwest of Porta de la Luz. It ran thus:

"Blown on our beam ends. Fear position hopeless. have already lost Maracot, Headley, Scanlan. Situation incomprehensible. Headley handkerchief end of deep sea sounding wire. God help us!

"S. S. *Stratford*."

This was the last incoherent message which came from the ill-fated vessel, and part of it was so strange that it was put down to delirium on the part of the operator. It seemed, however, to leave no doubt as to the fate of the ship.

The explanation—if it can be accepted as an explanation—of the matter is to be found in the narrative concealed inside the vitreous ball, and first it would be as well to amplify the very brief account which has hitherto appeared in the press of the finding of the ball. I take it verbatim from the log of the *Arabella Knowles*, master Amos Green, outward bound with coals from Cardiff to Buenos Aires:

"Wednesday, Jan. 5th, 1927. Lat. 27.14, Long. 28 West. Calm weather. Blue sky with low banks of cirrus clouds. Sea like glass. At two bells of the middle watch the first officer reported that he had seen a shining object bound high out of the sea, and then fall back into it. His first impression was that it was some strange fish, but on examination with his glasses he observed that it was a silvery globe, or ball, which was so light that it lay, rather than floated, on the surface of the water. I was called and saw it, as large as a football, gleaming brightly about half a mile off on our starboard beam. I stopped the engines and called away the quarter-boat under the second mate, who picked the thing up and brought it aboard.

"On examination it proved to be a ball made of some sort of very tough glass, and filled with a substance so light that when it was tossed in the air it wavered about like a child's balloon. It was nearly transparent, and we could see what looked like a roll of paper inside it. The material was so tough, however, that we had the greatest possible difficulty in breaking the ball open and getting at the contents. A hammer would not crack it, and it was only when the chief engineer nipped it in the throw of the engine that we were able to smash it. Then I am sorry to say that it dissolved into sparkling dust, so that it was impossible to collect any good sized piece for examination. We got the paper, however, and, having examined it and concluded that it was of great importance, we laid it aside with the intention of handing it over to the British Consul when we reached the Plate River. Man and boy, I have been at sea for five and thirty years, but this is the strangest thing that ever befell me, and so says every man aboard this ship. I leave the meaning of it all to wiser heads than mine."

So much for the genesis of the narrative of Cyrus J. Headley, which we will now give exactly as written:

Whom am I writing to? Well, I suppose I may say to the whole wide world, but as that is rather a vague address I'll aim at my friend Sir James Talbot, of Oxford University, for the reason that my last letter was to him and this may be regarded as a continuation. I expect the odds are a hundred to one that this ball, even if it should see the light of day and not be gulped by a shark in passing, will toss about on the waves and never catch the eye of the passing sailor, and yet it's worth trying, and Maracot is sending up another, so, between us, it may be that we shall get our wonderful story to the world. Whether the world will believe it is another matter, I guess, but when folk look at the ball with its vitrine cover and note its contents of levigen gas, they will surely see for themselves that there is something here that is out of the ordinary. You at any rate, Talbot, will not throw it aside, unread.

If anyone wants to know how the thing began, and what we were trying to do, he can find it all in a letter I wrote you on October 1st last year, the night before we left Porta de la Luz. By George! If I had known what was in store for us, I think I should have sneaked into a shore boat that night. And yet—well, maybe, even with my eyes open I would have stood by the Doctor and seen it through. On second thoughts I have not a doubt that I would.

Well, starting from the day we left Grand Canary I will carry on with my experiences.

The moment we were clear of the port, old man Maracot fairly broke into flames. The time for action had come at last and all the damped-down energy of the man came flaring up. I tell you he took hold of that ship and of everyone and everything in it, and bent it all to his will. The dry, creaking, absent-minded scholar had suddenly vanished, and instead there emerged a human electrical machine, crackling with vitality and quivering from the great driving force within. His eyes gleamed behind his glasses like flames in a lantern. He seemed to be everywhere at once, working out distances on his chart, comparing reckonings with the skipper, driving Bill Scanlan along, setting me on to a hundred odd jobs, but it was all full of method and with a definite end. He developed an unexpected knowledge of electricity and of mechanics and spent much of his time working at the machinery which Scanlan, under his supervision, was now carefully piecing together.

"Say, Mr. Headley, it's just dandy," said Bill, on the morning of the second day. "Come in here and have a look. The Doc is a regular fellow and a whale of a slick mechanic."

I had a most unpleasant impression that it was my own coffin at which I was gazing, but, even so, I had to admit that it was a very adequate mausoleum. The floor had been clamped to the four steel walls, and the porthole windows screwed into the centre of each. A small trap-door at the top gave admission, and there was a second one at the base. The steel cage was supported by a thin but very powerful steel hawser, which ran over a drum, and was paid out or rolled in by the strong engine which we used for our deep-sea trawls. The hawser, as I understood, was nearly half a mile in length, the slack of it coiled round bollards on the deck. The rubber breathing-tubes were of the same length, and the telephone wire was connected with them, and also the wire by which the electric lights within could be operated from the ship's batteries, though we had an independent instalment as well.

It was on the evening of that day that the engines were stopped. The glass was low, and a thick black cloud rising upon the horizon gave warning of coming trouble. The only ship in sight was a barque flying the Norwegian colours, and we observed that it was reefed down, as if expecting trouble. For the moment, however, all was propitious and the *Stratford* rolled gently upon a deep blue ocean, white-capped here and there from the breath of the trade wind. Bill Scanlan came to me in my laboratory with more show of excitement than his easy-going temperament had ever permitted him to show.

"Look it here, Mr. Headley," said he, "they've lowered that contraption into a well in the bottom of the ship. D'you figure that the Boss is going down it it?"

"Certain sure, Bill. And I am going with him."

"Well, well, you are sure bughouse, the two of you, to think of such a thing. But I'd feel a cheap skate if I let you go alone."

"It is no business of yours, Bill."

"Well, I just feel that it is. Sure, I'd be as yellow as a Chink with the jaundice if I let you go alone. Merribanks sent me here to look after the machinery, and if the machinery is down at the bottom of the sea, then it's a sure thing that it's me for the bottom. Where those steel casings are—that's the address of Bill Scanlan—whether the folk around him are crazy or no." It was useless to argue with him, so one more was added to our little suicide club and we just waited for our orders.

All night they were hard at work upon the fittings, and it was after an early breakfast that we descended into the hold ready for our adventure. The steel cage had been half-lowered into the false bottom, and we now descended one by one through the upper trapdoor, which was closed and screwed down behind us, Captain Howie with a most lugubrious face having shaken hands with each of us as we passed him. We were then lowered a few more feet, the shutter drawn above our heads, and the water admitted to test how far we were really seaworthy. The cage stood the trial well, every joint fitted exactly, and there was no sign of any leakage. Then the lower flap in the hold was loosened and we hung suspended in the ocean beneath the level of the keel.

It was really a very snug little room, and I marvelled at the skill and foresight with which everything had been arranged. The electric illumination had not been turned on, but the semi-tropical sun shone brightly through the bottle-green water at either porthole. Some small fish were flickering here and there, streaks of silver against the green background. Inside there was a settee round the little room, with a bathymetric dial, a thermometer, and other instruments ranged above it. Beneath the settee was a row of pipes which represented our reserve supply of compressed air in case the tubes should fail us. Those tubes opened out above our heads, and the telephonic apparatus hung beside them. We could all hear the mournful voice of the captain outside.

"Are you really determined to go?" he asked.

"We are quite all right," the Doctor answered impatiently. "You will lower slowly and have someone at the receiver all the time. I will report conditions. When we reach the bottom, remain as you are until I give instructions. It will not do to put too much strain upon the hawser, but a slow movement of a couple of knots an hour should be well within its strength. And now 'Lower away!'"

He yelled out the two words with the scream of a lunatic. It was the supreme moment of his life, the fruition of all his brooding dreams. For an instant I was shaken by the thought that we were really in the power of a cunning, plausible monomaniac. Bill Scanlan had the same thought, for he looked across at me with a rueful grin and touched his forehead. But after that one wild outburst our leader was instantly his sober, self-contained self once more. Indeed, one had but to look at the order and forethought which showed itself in every detail around us to be reassured as to the power of his mind.

But now all our attention was diverted to the wonderful new experience which every instant was providing. Slowly the cage was sinking into the depths of the ocean. Light green water turned to dark olive. That again deepened into a wonderful blue, a rich deep blue gradually thickening to a dusky purple. Lower and lower we sank—a hundred feet, two hundred feet, three hundred. The valves were acting to perfection. Our breathing was as free and natural as upon the deck of the vessel. Slowly the bathymeter needle moved round the luminous dial. Four hundred, five hundred, six hundred. "How are you?" roared an anxious voice from above us.

"Nothing could be better," cried Maracot in reply. But the light was failing. There was now only a dim gray twilight which rapidly changed to utter darkness. "Stop her!" shouted our leader. We ceased to move and hung suspended at seven hundred feet below the surface of the ocean. I heard the click of the switch, and the next instant we were flooded with glorious golden light which poured out through each of our side windows and sent long glimmering vistas into the waste of waters round us. With our faces against the thick glass, each at our own porthole, we gazed out into such a prospect as man had never seen.

Up to now we had known these strata by the sight of the few fish which had been too slow to avoid our clumsy trawl, or too stupid to escape a dragnet. Now we saw the wonderful world of water as it really was. If the object of creation was the production of man it is strange that the ocean is so much more populous than the land. Broadway on a Saturday night, Lombard Street on a weekday afternoon, are not more crowded than the great sea spaces which lay before us. We had passed those surface strata where fish are either colourless or of the true maritime tints of ultramarine above and silver below. Here there were creatures of every conceivable tint and form which pelagic life can show. Delicate leptocephali or eel larva shot like streaks of burnished silver across the tunnel of radiance. The slow snake-like form of muroena, the deep-sea lamprey, writhed and twisted by, or the black ceratia, all spikes and mouth, gaped foolishly back at our peering faces. Sometimes it was the squat cuttle-fish which drifted across and glanced at us with human, sinister eyes, sometimes it was some crystal-clear pelagic form of life, cystoma or glaucus, which lent a flower-like charm to the scene. One huge caranx, or horse mackerel, butted savagely again and again against our window until the dark shadow of a seven-foot shark came across him, and he vanished into the gaping jaws. Dr. Maracot sat entranced, his notebook upon his knee scribbling down his observations and keeping up a muttered monologue of scientific comment. "What's that? What's that?" I would hear. "Yes, yes, Chimoera mirabilis as taken by the Michael Sars. Dear me, there is lepidion, but a new species as I should judge. Observe that macrurus, Mr. Headley; its colouring is quite different to what we get in the net." Once only was he taken quite aback. It was when a long oval object shot with great speed past his window from above, and left a vibrating tail behind it which extended as far as we could see above us and below. I admit that I was as puzzled for the moment as the doctor, and it was Bill Scanlan who solved the mystery.

"I guess that boob, John Sweeney, has heaved his head alongside of us. Kind of a joke, maybe, to prevent us from feeling lonesome."

"To be sure! To be sure!" said Maracot, sniggering. "Plumbus longicaudatus—a new genus, Mr. Headley, with a piano-wire tail and lead in its nose. But, indeed, it is very necessary they should take soundings so as to keep above the bank, which is circumscribed in size. All well, Captain!" he shouted. "You may drop us down."

And down we went. Dr. Maracot turned off the electric light and all was pitch darkness once more save for the bathymeter's luminous face, which ticked off our steady fall. There was a gentle sway, but otherwise we were hardly conscious of any motion. Only that moving hand upon the dial told us of our terrific, our inconceivable, position. Now we were at the thousand-foot level, and the air had become distinctly foul. Scanlan oiled the valve of the discharge tube and things were better. At fifteen hundred feet we stopped and swung in mid-ocean with our lights blazing once more. Some great dark mass passed us here, but whether swordfish or deep-sea shark, or monster of unknown breed, was more than we could determine. The doctor hurriedly turned off the lights. "There lies our chief danger," said he; "there are creatures in the deep before whose charge this steel-plated room would have as much chance as a beehive before the rush of a rhinoceros."

"Whales, maybe," said Scanlan.

"Whales may sound to a great depth," the savant answered. "A Greenland whale has been known to take out nearly a mile of line in a perpendicular dive. But unless hurt or badly frightened no whale would descend so low. It may have been a giant squid. They are found at every level."

"Well, I guess squids are too soft to hurt us. The laugh would be with the squid if he could claw a hole in Merribank's nickel steel."

"Their bodies may be soft," the professor answered, "but the beak of a large squid would sheer through a bar of iron, and one peck of that beak might go through these inch-thick windows as if they were parchment."

"Gee Whittaker!" cried Bill, as we resumed our downward journey.

And then at last, quite softly and gently, we came to rest. So delicate was the impact that we should hardly have known of it had it not been that the light when turned on showed great coils of the hawser all around us. The wire was a danger to our breathing-tubes, for it might foul them, and at the urgent cry of Maracot it was pulled taut from above once more. The dial marked eighteen hundred feet. We lay motionless on a volcanic ridge at the bottom of the Atlantic.

CHAPTER II

For a time I think that we all had the same feeling. We did not want to do anything or to see anything. We just wanted to sit quiet and try to realize the wonder of it—that we should be resting in the plumb centre of one of the great oceans of the world. But soon the strange scene round us, illuminated in all directions by our lights, drew us to the windows.

We had settled upon a bed of high algae ("Cutleria multifida," said Maracot), the yellow fronds of which waved around us, moved by some deep-sea current, exactly as branches would move in a summer breeze. They were not long enough to obscure our view, though their great flat leaves, deep golden in the light, flowed occasionally across our vision. Beyond them lay slopes of some blackish slag-like material which were dotted with lovely coloured creatures, holothurians, ascidians, echini, and echinoderms, as thickly as ever an English spring-time bank was sprinkled with hyacinths and primroses. These living flowers of the sea, vivid scarlet, rich purple, and delicate pink, were spread in profusion upon that coal-black background. Here and there great sponges bristled out from the crevices of the dark rocks, and a few fish of the middle depths, themselves showing up as flashes of colour, shot across our circle of vivid radiance. We were gazing enraptured at the fairy scene when an anxious voice came down the tube:

"Well, how do you like the bottom? Is all well with you? Don't be too long, for the glass is dropping and I don't like the look of it. Giving you air enough? Anything more we can do?"

"All right, Captain!" cried Maracot cheerily. "We won't be long. You are nursing us well. We are quite as comfortable as in our own cabin. Stand by presently to move us slowly forward."

We had come into the region of the luminous fishes, and it amused us to turn out our own lights, and in the absolute pitch darkness—a darkness in which a sensitive plate can be suspended for an hour without a trace even of the ultra-violet ray—to look out at the phosphorescent activity of the ocean. As against a black velvet curtain one saw little points of brilliant light moving steadily along as a liner at night might shed light through its long line of portholes. One terrifying creature had luminous teeth which gnashed in Biblical fashion in the outer darkness. Another had long golden antennae, and yet another a plume of flame above its head. As far as our vision carried, brilliant points flashed in the darkness, each little being bent upon its own business, and lighting up its own course as surely as the nightly taxicab at the theatre-hour in the Strand. Soon we had our own lights up again and the Doctor was making his observations of the sea bottom.

"Deep as we are, we are not deep enough to get any of the characteristic bathic deposits," said he. "These are entirely beyond our possible range. Perhaps on another occasion with a longer hawser——"

"Cut it out!" growled Bill. "Forget it!"

Maracot smiled. "You will soon get acclimated to the depths, Scanlan. This will not be our only descent."

"The hell you say!" muttered Bill.

"You will think no more of it than of going down into the hold of the *Stratford*. You will observe, Mr. Headley, that the groundwork here, so far as we can observe it through the dense growth of hydrozoa and silicious sponges, is pumice stone and the black slag of basalt, pointing to ancient plutonic activities. Indeed, I am inclined to think that it confirms my previous view that this ridge is part of a volcanic formation and that the Maracot Deep," he rolled out the words as if he loved them, "represents the outer slope of the mountain. It has struck me that it would be an interesting experiment to move our cage slowly onward until we come to the edge of the Deep, and see exactly what the formation may be at that point. I should expect to find a precipice of majestic dimensions extending downward at a sharp angle into the extreme depths of the ocean."

The experiment seemed to me to be a dangerous one, for who could say how far our thin hawser could bear the strain of lateral movement; but with Maracot danger, either to himself or to anyone else, simply did not exist when a scientific observation had to be made. I held my breath, and so I observed did Bill Scanlan, when a slow movement of our steel shell, brushing aside the waving fronds of seaweed, showed that the full strain was upon the line. It stood it nobly, however, and with a very gentle sweeping progression we began to glide over the bottom of the ocean, Maracot, with a compass in the hollow of his hand, shouting his direction as to the course to follow, and occasionally ordering the shell to be raised so as to avoid some obstacle in our path.

"This basaltic ridge can hardly be more than a mile

across," he explained. "I had marked the abyss as being to the west of the point where we took our plunge. At this rate, we should certainly reach it in a very short time."

We slid without any check over the volcanic plain, all feathered by the waving golden algae and made beautiful by the gorgeous jewels of Nature's cutting, flaming out from their setting of jet. Suddenly the Doctor dashed to the telephone.

"Stop her!" he cried. "We are there!"

A monstrous gap had opened suddenly before us. It was a fearsome place, the vision of a nightmare. Black shining cliffs of basalt fell sheer down into the unknown. Their edges were fringed with dangling laminaria as ferns might overhang some earthly gorge, but beneath that tossing, vibrating rim there were only the black gleaming walls of the chasm. The rocky edge curved away from us, but the abyss might be of any breadth, for our lights failed to penetrate the gloom which lay before us. When a Lucas signalling lamp was turned downward it shot out a long golden lane of parallel beams extending down, down, down until it was quenched in the gloom of the terrible chasm beneath us.

"It is indeed wonderful!" cried Maracot, gazing out with a pleased proprietary expression upon his thin, eager face. "For depth I need not say that it has often been exceeded. There is the Challenger Deep of twenty-six thousand feet near the Ladrone Islands, the Planet Deep of thirty-two thousand feet off the Philippines, and many others, but it is probable that the Maracot Deep stands alone in the declivity of its descent, and is remarkable also for its escape from the observation of so many hydrographic explorers who have charted the Atlantic. It can hardly be doubted——"

He had stopped in the middle of a sentence and a look of intense interest and surprise had frozen upon his face. Bill Scanlan and I gazing over his shoulders, were petrified by that which met our startled eyes.

Some great creatre was coming up the tunnel of light which we had projected into the abyss. Far down where it tailed off into the darkness of the pit we could dimly see the vague black lurchings and heavings of some monstrous body in slow upward progression. Paddling in clumsy fashion, it was rising with dim flickerings to the edge of the gulf. Now, as it came nearer, it was right in the beam, and we could see its dreadful form more clearly. It was a beast unknown to Science, and yet with an analogy to much with which we are familiar. Too long for a huge crab and too short for a giant lobster, it was moulded more upon the lines of the crayfish, with two monstrous nippers outstretched on either side, and a pair of sixteen-foot antennae which quivered in front of its black, dull, sullen eyes. The carapace, light yellow in colour, may have been ten feet across, and its total length, apart from the antennae, must have been not less than thirty.

"Wonderful!" cried Maracot, scribbling desperately in his notebook. "Semi-pediculated eyes, elastic lamelae, family crustaceae, species unknown. Crustaceus Maracoti—why not? Why not?"

"By gosh, I'll pass its name, but it seems to me it's coming our way!" cried Bill. "Say, Doc, what about putting our light out?"

"Just one moment while I note the reticulations!" cried the naturalist. "Yes, yes, that will do." He clicked off the switch and we were back in our inky darkness, with only the darting lights outside like meteors on a moonless night.

"That beast is sure the world's worst," said Bill, wiping his forehead. "I felt like the morning after a bottle of Prohibition Hooch."

"It is certainly terrible to look at," Maracot remarked, "and perhaps terrible to deal with also if we were really exposed to those monstrous claws. But inside our steel case we can afford to examine him in safety and at our ease."

He had hardly spoken when there came a rap as from a pickaxe upon our outer wall. Then there was a long-drawn rasping and scratching, ending in another sharp rap.

"Say, he wants to come in!" cried Bill Scanlan in alarm. "By gosh we want 'No Admission' painted on this shack." His shaking voice showed how forced was his merriment, and I confess that my own knees were knocking together as I was aware of the stealthy monster closing up with an even blacker darkness each of our windows in succession, as he explored this strange shell which could he but crack it, might contain his food.

"He can't hurt us," said Maracot, but there was less assurance in his tone. "Maybe it would be as well to shake the brute off." He hailed the Captain up the tube.

"Pull us up twenty or thirty feet," he cried.

A few seconds later we rose from the lava plain and swung gently in the still water. But the terrible beast was pertinacious. After a very short interval we heard once more the raspings of his feelers and the sharp tappings of his claws as he felt us round. It was terrible to sit silently in the dark and know that death was so near. If that mighty claw fell upon the window, would it stand the strain? That was the unspoken question in each of our minds.

But suddenly an unexpected and more urgent danger presented itself. The tappings had gone to the roof of our little dwelling, and now we began to sway with a rhythmic movement to and fro.

"Good God!" I cried. "It has hold of the hawser. It will surely snap it."

"Say, Doc, it's mine for the surface. I guess we've seen what we came to see, and it's home, sweet home for Bill Scanlan. Ring up the elevator and get her going."

"But our work is not half done," croaked Maracot. "We have only begun to explore the edges of the Deep. Let us at least see how broad it is. When we have reached the other side I shall be content to return." Then up the tube: "All well, Captain. Move on at two knots until I call for a stop."

We moved slowly out over the edge of the abyss. Since darkness had not saved us from attack we now turned on our lights. One of the portholes was entirely obscured by what appeared to be the creature's lower stomach. Its head and its great nippers were at work above us, and we still swayed like a clanging bell. The strength of the beast must have been enormous. Were ever mortals placed in such a situation, with five miles of water beneath—and that deadly monster above? The oscillations became more and more violent. An excited shout came down the tube from the Captain as he became aware of the jerks upon the hawser, and Maracot sprang to his feet with his hands thrown upwards in despair. Even within the shell we were aware of the jar of the broken wires, and an instant later we were falling into the mighty gulf beneath us.

As I look back at that awful moment I can remember hearing a wild cry from Maracot.

"The hawser has parted! You can do nothing! We are all dead men!" he yelled, grabbing at the telephone tube, and then, "Good-bye, Captain, good-bye to all." They were our last words to the world of men.

We did not fall swiftly down, as you might have imagined. In spite of our weight our hollow shell gave us some sustaining buoyancy, and we sank slowly and gently into the abyss. I heard the long scrape as we slid through the claws of the horrible creature who had been our ruin, and then with a smooth gyration we went circling downwards into the abysmal depths. It may have been fully five minutes, and it seemed like an hour, before we reached the limit of our telephone wire and snapped it like a thread. Our air tube broke off at almost the same moment and the salt water came spouting through the vents. With quick, deft hands Bill Scanlan tied cords round each of the rubber tubes and so stopped the inrush, while the Doctor released the top of our compressed air which came hissing forth from the tubes. The lights had gone out when the wire snapped, but even in the dark the Doctor was able to connect up the Hellesens dry cells which lit a number of lamps in the roof.

"It should last us a week," he said, with a wry smile. "We shall at least have light to die in." Then he shook his head sadly and a kindly smile came over his gaunt features. "It is all right for me. I am an old man and have done my work in the world. My one regret is that I should have allowed you two young fellows to come with me. I should have taken the risk alone."

I simply shook his hand in reassurance, for indeed there was nothing I could say. Bill Scanlan, too, was silent. Slowly we sank, marking our pace by the dark fish shadows which flitted past our windows. It seemed as if they were flying upwards rather than that we were sinking down. We still oscillated, and there was nothing so far as I could see to prevent us from falling on our side, or even turning upside down. Our weight, however, was, fortunately, very evenly balanced and we kept a level floor. Glancing up at the bathymeter I saw that we had already reached the depth of a mile.

"You see, it is as I said," remarked Maracot with some complacency. "You may have seen my paper in the Proceedings of the Oceanographical Society upon the relation of pressure and depth. I wish I could get one word back to the world, if only to confute Bülow of Giessen, who ventured to contradict me."

"My gosh! If I could get a word back to the world I wouldn't waste it on a square-head highbrow," said the mechanic. "There is a little wren in Philadelphia that will have tears in her pretty eyes when she hears that Bill Scanlan has passed out. Well, it sure does seem a dumb queer way of doing it, anyhow."

"You should never have come," I said, putting my hand on his.

"What sort of tin-horn sport should I have been if I had quitted?" he answered. "No, it's my job, and I am glad I stuck it."

"How long have we?" I asked the Doctor, after a pause.

He shrugged his shoulders.

"We shall have time to see the real bottom of the ocean, anyhow," said he. "There is air enough in our tubes for the best part of a day. Our trouble is with the waste products. That is what is going to choke us. If we could get rid of our carbon dioxide——"

"That I can see is impossible."

"There is one tube of pure oxygen. I put it in in case of accidents. A little of that from time to time will help to keep us alive. You will observe that we are now more than two miles deep."

"Why should we try to keep ourselves alive? The sooner it is over the better," said I.

"That's the dope," cried Scanlan. "Cut loose and have done with it."

"And miss the most wonderful sight that man's eye has ever seen!" said Maracot. "It would be treason to Science. Let us record facts to the end, even if they should be forever buried with our bodies. Play the game out."

"Some sport, the Doc!" cried Scanlan. "I guess he

has the best guts of the bunch. Let us see the spiel to an end."

We sat patiently on the settee, the three of us, gripping the edges of it with strained fingers as it swayed and rocked, while the fishes still flashed swiftly upwards athwart the portholes.

"It is now three miles," remarked Maracot. "I will turn on the oxygen, Mr. Headley, for it is certainly very close. There is one thing," he added, with his dry, cackling laugh. "It will certainly be the Maracot Deep from this time onwards. When Captain Howie takes back the news my colleagues will see to it that my grave is also my monument. Even Bülow of Giessen——" He babbled on about some unintelligible scientific grievance.

We sat in silence again, watching the needle as it crawled on to its fourth mile. At one point we struck something heavy, which shook us so violently that I feared that we would turn upon our side. It may have been a huge fish, or conceivably we may have bumped upon some projection of the cliff over the edge of which we had been precipitated. That edge had seemed to us at the time to be such a wondrous depth, and now looking back at it from our dreadful abyss it might almost have been the surface. Still we swirled and circled lower and lower through the dark green waste of waters. Twenty-five thousand feet now was registered upon the dial.

"We are nearly at our journey's end," said Maracot. "My Scott's recorder gave me twenty-six thousand seven hundred last year at the deepest point. We shall know our fate within a few minutes. It may be that the shock will crush us. It may be——"

And at that moment we landed.

There was never a babe lowered by its mother on to a feather bed who nestled down more gently than we on to the extreme bottom of the Atlantic Ocean.

The soft, thick, elastic ooze upon which we lit was a perfect buffer, which saved us from the slightest jar. We hardly moved upon our seats, and it as well that we did not, for we had perched upon some sort of a projecting hummock, clothed thickly with the viscous gelatinous mud, and there we were balanced rocking gently with nearly half our base projecting and unsupported. There was a danger that we would tip over on our side, but finally we steadied down and remained motionless. As we did so Dr. Maracot, staring out through his porthole, gave a cry of surprise and hurriedly turned out our electric light.

To our amazement we could still see clearly. There was a dim, misty light outside which streamed through our porthole, like the cold radiance of a winter morning. We looked out at the strange scene, and with no help from our own lights we could see clearly for some hundred yards in each direction. It was impossible, inconceivable, but none the less the evidence of our senses told us that it was a fact. The great ocean floor is luminous.

"Why not?" cried Maracot, when we had stood for a minute or two in silent wonder. "Should I not have foreseen it? What is this pteropod or blobigerina ooze? It is not the product of decay, the mouldering bodies of a billion billion organic creatures? And is decay not associated with phosphorescent luminosity? Where, in all creation, would it be seen if it were not here? Ah! it is indeed hard that we should have such a demonstration and be unable to send our knowledge back to the world."

"And yet," I remarked, "we have scooped half a ton of radiolarian jelly at a time and detected no such radiance."

"It would lose it, doubtless, in its long journey to the surface. And what is half a ton compared to these far-stretching plains of slow putrescence? And see,

see," he cried in uncontrollable excitement, "the deep-sea creatures graze upon this organic carpet even as our herds on land graze upon the meadows!"

As he spoke a flock of big black fish, heavy and squat, came slowly over the ocean bed towards us, nuzzling among the spongy growths and nibbling away as they advanced. Another huge red creature, like a foolish cow of the ocean, was chewing the cud in front of my porthole and others were grazing here and there, raising their heads from time to time to gaze at this strange object which had so suddenly appeared among them.

I could only marvel at Maracot, who in that foul atmosphere, seated under the very shadow of death, still obeyed the call of Science and scribbled his observations in his notebook. Without following his precise methods, I none the less made my own mental notes, which will remain forever as a picture stamped upon my brain. The lowest plains of ocean consist of red clay, but here it was overlaid by the gray bathybian slime which formed an undulating plain as far as our eyes could reach. This plain was not smooth, but was broken by numerous strange rounded hillocks like that upon which we had perched, all glimmering in the spectral light. Between these little hills there darted great clouds of strange fish, many of them quite unknown to Science, exhibiting every shade of colour, but black and red predominating. Maracot watched them with suppressed excitement and chronicled them in his notes.

The air had become very foul, and again we were only able to save ourselves by a fresh emission of oxygen. Curiously enough, we were all hungry—I should rather say ravenous—and we fell upon the potted beef with bread and butter, washed down by whisky and water, which the foresight of Maracot had provided. With my perceptions stimulated by this refreshment, I was seated at my look-out portal and longing for a last cigarette, when my eyes caught something which sent a whirl of strange thoughts and anticipations through my mind.

I have said that the undulating gray plain on every side of us was studded with what seemed like hummocks. A particularly large one was in front of my porthole, and I looked out at it within a range of thirty feet. There was some peculiar mark upon the side of it, and as I glanced along I saw to my surprise that this mark was repeated again and again until it was lost round the curve. When one is so near death it takes much to give one a thrill about anything connected with this world, but my breath failed me for a moment and my heart stood still as I suddenly realized that it was a frieze at which I was looking and that, barnacled and worn as it was, the hand of man had surely at some time carved these faded figures. Maracot and Scanlan crowded to my porthole and gazed out in utter amazement at these signs of the omnipresent energies of man.

"It is carving, for sure!" cried Scanlan. "I guess this dump has been the roof of a building. Then these other ones are buildings also. Say, boss, we've dropped plumb on to a regular burg."

"It is, indeed, an ancient city," said Maracot. "Geology teaches that the seas have once been continents and the continents seas, but I have always distrusted the idea that in times so recent as the quaternary there could have been an Atlantic subsidence. Plato's report of Egyptian gossip had then a foundation of fact. These volcanic formations confirm the view that this subsidence was due to seismic activity."

"There is regularity about these domes," I remarked. "I begin to think that they are not separate houses, but that they are cupolas and form the ornaments of the roof of some huge building."

"I guess you are right," said Scanlan. "There are four big ones at the corners and the small ones in lines between. It's some building, if we could see the whole of it! You could put the whole Merribank plant inside it—and then some."

"It has been buried up to the roof by the constant dropping from above," said Maracot. "On the other hand, it has not decayed. We have a constant temperature of a little over 32° Fahrenheit in the great depths, which would arrest destructive processes. Even the dissolution of the bathic remains which pave the floor of the ocean and incidentally give us this luminosity must be a very slow one. But, dear me! this marking is not a frieze but an inscription."

There was no doubt that he was right. The same symbol recurred every here and there. These marks were unquestionably letters of some archaic alphabet.

"I have made a study of Phoenician antiquities, and there is certainly something suggestive and familiar in these characters," said our leader. "Well, we have seen a buried city of ancient days, my friends, and we carry a wonderful piece of knowledge with us to the grave. There is no more to be learned. Our book of knowledge is closed. I agree with you that the sooner the end comes the better."

It could not now be long delayed. The air was stagnant and dreadful. So heavy was it with carbon products that the oxygen could hardly force its way out against the pressure. By standing on the settee one was able to get a gulp of purer air, but the mephitic reek was slowly rising. Dr. Maracot folded his arms with an air of resignation and sank his head upon his breast. Scanlan was now overpowered by the fumes and was already sprawling upon the floor. My own head was swimming, and I felt an intolerable weight at my chest. I closed my eyes and my senses were rapidly slipping away. Then I opened them for one last glimpse of that world which I was leaving, and as I did so I staggered to my feet with a hoarse scream of amazement.

A human face was looking in at us through the porthole.

Was it my delirium? I clutched at the shoulder of Maracot and shook him violently. He sat up and stared, wonderstruck and speechless, at this apparition. If he saw it as well as I, it was no figment of the brain. The face was long and thin, dark in complexion, with a short pointed beard, and two vivid eyes darting here and there in quick, questioning glances which took in every detail of our situation. The utmost amazement was visible upon the man's face. Our lights were now full on, and it must indeed have been a strange and vivid picture which presented itself to his gaze in that tiny chamber of death, where one man lay senseless and two others glared out at him with the twisted, contorted features of dying men, cyanosed by incipient asphyxiation. We both had our hands to our throats, and our heaving chests carried their message of despair. The man gave a wave of his hand and hurried away.

"He has deserted us!" cried Maracot.

"Or gone for help. Let us get Scanlan on the couch. It's death for him down there."

We dragged the mechanic on to the settee and propped his head against the cushions. His face was gray and he murmured in delirium, but his pulse was still perceptible.

"There is hope for us yet," I croaked.

"But it is madness!" cried Maracot. "How can man live at the bottom of the ocean? How can he breathe? It is collective hallucination. My young friend, we are going mad."

Looking out at the bleak, lonely gray landscape in the dreary spectral light, I felt that it might be as

Maracot said. Then suddenly I was aware of movement. Shadows were flitting through the distant water. They hardened and thickened into moving figures. A crowd of people were hurrying across the ocean bed in our direction. An instant later they had assembled in front of the porthole and were pointing and gesticulating in animated debate. There were several women in the crowd, but the greater part were men, one of whom, a powerful figure with a very large head and a full black beard, was clearly a person of authority. He made a swift inspection of our steel shell, and, since the edge of our base projected over the place on which we rested, he was able to see that there was a hinged trapdoor at the bottom. He now sent a messenger flying back, while he made energetic and commanding signs to us to open the door from within.

"Why not?" I asked. "We may as well be drowned as be smothered. I can stand it no longer."

"We may not be drowned," said Maracot. "The water entering from below cannot rise above the level of the compressed air. Give Scanlan some brandy. He must make an effort, if it is his last one."

I forced a drink down the mechanic's throat. He gulped and looked round him with wondering eyes. Between us we got him erect on the settee and stood on either side of him. He was still half-dazed, but in a few words I explained the situation.

"There is a chance of chlorine poisoning if the water reaches the batteries," said Maracot. "Open every air tube, for the more pressure we can get the less water may enter. Now help me while I pull upon the lever."

We bent our weight upon it and yanked up the circular plate from the bottom of our little home, though I felt like a suicide as I did so. The green water, sparkling and gleaming under our light, came gurgling and surging in. It rose rapidly to our feet, to our knees, to our waists, and there it stopped. But the pressure of air was intolerable. Our heads buzzed and the drums of our ears were bursting. We could not have lived in such an atmosphere for long. Only by clutching at the rack could we save ourselves from falling back into the waters beneath us.

From our higher position we could no longer see through the portholes, nor could we imagine what steps were being taken for our deliverance. Indeed, that any effective help could come to us seemed beyond the power of thought, and yet there was a commanding and purposeful air about these people, and especially about that squat bearded chieftain, which inspired vague hopes. Suddenly we were aware of his face looking up at us through the water beneath and an instant later he had passed through the circular opening and had clambered on to the settee, so that he was standing by our side—a short, sturdy figure, not higher than my shoulder, but surveying us with large brown eyes, which were full of a half-amused confidence, as who should say, "You poor devils; you think you are in a very bad way, but I can clearly see the road out."

Only now was I aware of a very amazing thing. The man, if indeed he was of the same humanity as ourselves, had a transparent envelope all round him which enveloped his head and body, while his arms and legs were free. So translucent was it that no one could detect it in the water, but now that he was in the air beside us it glistened like silver, though it remained as clear as the finest glass. On either shoulder he had a curious rounded projection beneath the clear protective sheath. It looked like an oblong box pierced with many holes, and gave him an appearance as if he were wearing epaulettes.

When our new friend had joined us another face

appeared in the aperture of the bottom and thrust through it what seemed like a great bubble of glass. Three of these in succession were passed in and floated upon the surface of the water. Then six small boxes were handed up and our new acquaintance tied one with the straps attached to them to each of our shoulders, whence they stood up like his own. And already I began to surmise that no infraction of natural law was involved in the life of these strange people, and that while one box in some new fashion was a producer of air the other was an absorber of waste products. He now passed the transparent suits over our heads, and we felt that they clasped us tightly in the upper arm and waist by elastic bands, so that no water could penetrate. Within we breathed with perfect ease, and it was a joy to me to see Maracot looking out at me with his eyes twinkling as of old behind his glasses, while Bill Scanlan's grin assured me that the life-giving oxygen had done its work, and that he was his cheerful self once more. Our rescuer looked from one to another of us with grave satisfaction, and then motioned to us to follow him through the trap-door and out on to the floor of the ocean. A dozen willing hands were outstretched to pull us through and to sustain our first faltering steps as we staggered with our feet deep in the slimy ooze.

Even now I cannot get past the marvel of it! There we were, the three of us, unhurt and at our ease at the bottom of a five-mile abyss of water. Where was that terrific pressure which had exercised the imagination of so many scientists? We were no more affected by it than were the dainty fish which swam around us. It is true that, so far as our bodies were concerned, we were protected by these delicate bells of vitrine, which were in truth tougher than the strongest steel, but even our limbs, which were exposed, felt no more than a firm constriction from the water which one learned in time to disregard. It was wonderful to stand together and to look back at the shell from which we had emerged. We had left the batteries at work, and it was a wondrous object with its streams of yellow light flooding out from each side, while clouds of fishes gathered at each window. As we watched it the leader took Maracot by the hand, and we followed them both across the watery morass, clumping heavily through the sticky surface.

And now a most surprising incident occurred, which was clearly as astonishing to these strange new companions of ours as to ourselves. Above our heads there appeared a small, dark object, descending from the darkness above us and swinging down until it reached the bed of the ocean within a very short distance from where we stood. It was, of course, the deep-sea lead from the *Stratford* above us, making a sounding of that water gulf with which the name of the expedition was to be associated. We had seen it already upon its downward path, and we could well understand that the tragedy of our disappearance had suspended the operation, but that after a pause it had been concluded, with little thought that it would finish almost at our feet. They were unconscious, apparently, that they had touched bottom, for the lead lay motionless in the ooze. Above me stretched the taut piano wire which connected me through five miles of water with the deck of our vessel. Oh, that it were possible to write a note and to attach it! The idea was absurd, and yet could I not send some message which would show them that we were still conscious? My coat was covered by my glass bell and the pockets were unapproachable, but I was free below the waist and my handkerchief chanced to be in my trousers pocket. I pulled it out and tied it above the top of the lead. The weight itself at once disengaged itself by its automatic mechanism, and presently I saw my white wisp of linen flying upwards to that world which I may never see again. Our new acquaintances examined the seventy-five pounds of lead with great interest, and finally carried it off with us as we went upon our way.

We had only walked a couple of hundred yards, threading our way among the hummocks, when we halted before a small square-cut door with solid pillars on either side and an inscription across the lintel. It was open, and we passed through it into a large, bare chamber. There was a sliding partition worked by a crank from within, and this was drawn across behind us. We could, of course, hear nothing in our glass helmets, but after standing a few minutes we were aware that a powerful pump must be at work, for we saw the level of the water sinking rapidly above us. In less than a quarter of an hour we were standing upon a sloppy stone-flagged pavement, while our new friends were busy in undoing the fastenings of our transparent suits. An instant later there we stood, breathing perfectly pure air in a warm, well-lighted atmosphere, while the dark people of the abyss, smiling and chattering, crowded round us with hand-shakings and friendly pattings. It was a strange, rasping tongue that they spoke, and no word of it was intelligible to us, but the smile on the face and the light of friendship in the eye are understandable even in the waters under the earth. The glass suits were hung on numbered pegs upon the wall, and the kindly folk half-led and half-pushed us to an inner door which opened onto a long downward-sloping corridor. When it closed again behind us there was nothing to remind us of the stupendous fact that we were the involuntary guests of an unknown race at the bottom of the Atlantic Ocean and cut off forever from the world to which we belonged.

Now that the terrific strain had been so suddenly

eased we were all exhausted. Even Bill Scanlan, who was a pocket Hercules, dragged his feet along the floor, while Maracot and I were only too glad to lean heavily upon our guides. Yet, weary as I was, I took in every detail as we passed. That the air came from some air-making machine was very evident, for it issued in puffs from circular openings in the walls. The light was diffused and was clearly an extension of that fluor system which was already engaging the attention of our European engineers when the filament and lamp were dispensed with. It shone from long cylinders of clear glass which were suspended along the cornices of the passages. So much I had observed when our descent was checked and we were ushered into a large sitting-room, thickly carpeted and well furnished with gilded chairs and sloping sofas which brought back vague memories of Egyptian tombs. The crowd had been dismissed and only the bearded man with two attendants remained. "Manda," he repeated several times, tapping himself upon the chest. Then he pointed to each of us in turn and repeated the words Maracot, Headley, and Scanlan until he had them perfect. He then motioned us to be seated and said a word to one of the attendants, who left the room and returned presently, escorting a very ancient gentleman, white-haired and long-bearded, with a curious conical cap of black cloth upon his head. I should have said that all these folk were dressed in coloured tunics, which extended to their knees, with high boots of fish skin or shagreen. The venerable newcomer was clearly a physician, for he examined each of us in turn, placing his hand upon our brows and closing his own eyes as if receiving a mental impression as to our condition. Apparently he was by no means satisfied, for he shook his head and said a few grave words to Manda. The latter at once sent the attendant out once more, and he brought in a tray of eatables and a flask of wine, which were laid before us. We were too weary to ask ourselves what they were, but we felt the better for the meal. We were then led to another room, where three beds had been prepared, and on one of these I flung myself down. I have a dim recollection of Bill Scanlan coming across and sitting beside me.

"Say, Bo, that jolt of brandy saved my life," cried he. "But where are we, anyhow?"

"I know no more than you do."

"Well, I am ready to hit the hay," he said, sleepily, as he turned to his bed. "Say, that wine was fine. Thank God, Volstead never got down here." They were the last words I heard as I sank into the most profound sleep that I can ever recall.

CHAPTER III

When I came to myself I could not at first imagine where I was. The events of the previous day were like some blurred nightmare, and I could not believe that I had to accept them as facts. I looked round in bewilderment at the large, bare, windowless room with drab-coloured walls, at the lines of quivering purplish light which flowed along the cornices, at the scattered articles of furniture, and finally at the two other beds, from one of which came the high-pitched strident snore which I had learned, aboard the *Stratford*, to associate with Maracot. It was too grotesque to be true, and it was only when I fingered my bed cover and observed the curious woven material, and dried fibres of some sea plant, from which it was made, that I was able to realize this inconceivable adventure which had befallen us. I was still pondering it when there came a loud explosion of laughter, and Bill Scanlan sat up in bed.

"Mornin', Bo!" he cried, amid his chuckles, on seeing that I was awake.

"You seem in good spirits," said I, rather testily. "I can't see that we have much to laugh about."

"Well, I had a grouch on me, the same as you, when first I woke up," he answered. "Then came a real cute idea, and it was that that made me laugh."

"I could do with a laugh myself," said I. "What's the idea?"

"Well, Bo, I thought how durned funny it would have been if we had all tied ourselves on to that deep-sea line. I allow with those glass ginguses we could have kept breathing all right. Then when old man Howie looked over the side there would have been the whole bunch of us comin' up at him through the water. He would have figured that he had hooked us, sure. Gee, what a spiell!"

Our united laughter woke the Doctor, who sat up in bed with the same amazed expression upon his face which had previously been upon my own. I forgot our troubles as I listened in amusement to his disjointed comments, which alternated between ecstatic joy at the prospect of such a field of study, and profound sorrow that he could never hope to convey his results to his scientific *confrères* of the earth. Finally he got back to the actual needs of the moment.

"It is nine o'clock," he said, looking at his watch. We all registered the same hour, but there was nothing to show if it was night or morning.

"We must keep our own calendar," said Maracot; "we descended upon October 3rd. We reached this place on the evening of the same day. How long have we slept?"

"My gosh, it may have been a month," said Scanlan, "I've not been so deep since Mickey Scott got me on the point in the six-round try-out at the Works."

We dressed and washed, for every civilized convenience was at hand. The door, however, was fastened, and it was clear that we were prisoners for the time. In spite of the apparent absence of any ventilation, the atmosphere kept perfectly sweet, and we found that this was due to a current of air which came through small holes in the wall. There was some source of central heating, too, for though no stove was visible, the temperature was pleasantly warm. Presently I observed a knob upon one of the walls, and pressed it. This was, as I expected, a bell, for the door instantly opened, and a small, dark man, dressed in a yellow robe, appeared in the aperture. He looked at us inquiringly, with large, brown, kindly eyes.

"We are hungry," said Maracot; "can you get us some food?"

The man shook his head and smiled. It was clear that the words were incomprehensible to him.

Scanlan tried his luck with a flow of American slang, which was received with the same blank smile. When, however, I opened my mouth and thrust my finger into it, our visitor nodded vigorously and hurried away.

Ten minutes later the door opened and two of the yellow attendants appeared, rolling a small table before them. Had we been at the Biltmore Hotel we could not have had better fare. There were coffee, hot milk, rolls, delicious flat fish, and honey. For half an hour we were far too busy to discuss what we ate or whence it was obtained. At the end of that time the two servants appeared once more, rolled out the tray, and closed the door carefully behind them.

"I'm fair black and blue with pinching myself," said Scanlan. "Is this a pipe dream or what? Say, Doc, you got us down here, and I guess it is up to you to tell us just how you size it all up."

The Doctor shook his head.

"It is like a dream to me also, but it is a glorious dream! What a story for the world if we could but get it to them!"

"One thing is clear," said I, "there was certainly truth in this legend of Atlantis, and some of the folk have in a marvellous way managed to carry on."

"Well, even if they carried on," cried Bill Scanlan, scratching his bullet head, "I am darned if I can understand how they could get air and fresh water and the rest. Maybe if that queer duck with the beard that we saw last night comes to give us a once-over he will put us wise to it."

"How can he do that when we have no common language?"

"Well, we shall use our own observation," said Maracot. "One thing I can already understand. I learned it from the honey at breakfast. That was clearly synthetic honey, such as we have already learned to make upon the earth. But if synthetic honey, why not synthetic coffee, or flour? The molecules of the elements are like bricks, and these bricks lie all around us. We have only to learn how to pull out certain bricks—sometimes just a single brick—in order to make a fresh substance. Sugar becomes starch, or either becomes alcohol, just by a shifting of the bricks. What is it that shifts them? Heat. Electricity. Other things perhaps of which we know nothing. Some of them will shift themselves, and radium becomes lead or uranium becomes radium without our touching them."

"You think, then, that they have an advanced chemistry?"

"I'm sure of it. After all, there is no elemental brick which is not ready to their hands. Hydrogen and oxygen come readily from the sea water. There are nitrogen and carbon in those masses of sea vegetation, and there are phosphorus and calcium in the bathybic deposit. With skilful management and adequate knowledge what is there which could not be produced?"

The Doctor had launched upon a chemical lecture when the door opened and Manda entered, giving us a friendly greeting. There came with him the same old gentleman of venerable appearance whom we had met the night before. He may have had a reputation for learning, for he tried several sentences, which were probably different languages, upon us, but all were equally unintelligible. Then he shrugged his shoulders and spoke to Manda, who gave an order to the two yellow-clad servants, still waiting at the door. They vanished, but returned presently with a curious screen, supported by two side posts. It was exactly like one of our cinema screens, but it was coated with some sparkling material which glittered and shimmered in the light. This was placed against one of the walls. The old man then paced out very carefully a certain distance, and marked it upon the floor. Standing at this point he turned to Maracot and touched his forehead, pointing to the screen.

"Clean dippy," said Scanlan. "Bats in the belfrey."

Maracot shook his head to show that we were nonplussed. So was the old man for a moment. An idea struck him, however, and he pointed to his own figure. Then he turned towards the screen, fixed his eyes upon it, and seemed to concentrate his attention. In an instant a reflection of himself appeared on the screen before us. Then he pointed to us, and a moment later our own little group took the place of his image. It was not particularly like us. Scanlan looked like a comic Chinaman and Maracot like a decayed corpse, but it was clearly meant to be ourselves as we appeared in the eyes of the operator.

"It's a reflection of thought," I cried.

"Exactly," said Maracot. "This is certainly a most marvellous invention, and yet it is but a combination of such telepathy and television as we dimly comprehend upon earth."

"I never thought I'd live to see myself in the movies, if that cheese-faced Chink is really meant for me," said Scanlan. "Say, if we could get all this news to the editor of the *Ledger* he'd cough up enough to keep me for life. We've sure got the goods if we could deliver them."

"That's the trouble," said I. "By George, we could stir the whole world if we could only get back to it. But what is he beckoning about?"

"The old guy wants you to try your hand at it, Doc."

Maracot took the place indicated, and his strong, clear-cut brain focussed his picture to perfection. We saw an image of Manda, and then another one of the *Stratford* as we had left her.

Both Manda and the old scientist nodded their great approval at the sight of the ship, and Manda made a sweeping gesture with his hands, pointing first to us and then to the screen.

"To tell them all about it—that's the idea," I cried. "They want to know in pictures who we are, and how we got here."

Maracot nodded to Manda to show that he understood, and had begun to throw an image of our voyage, when Manda held up his hand and stopped him. At an order the attendants removed the screen, and the two Atlanteans beckoned that we should follow them.

It was a huge building, and we proceeded down corridor after corridor until we came at last to a large hall with seats arranged in tiers like a lecture room. At one side was a broad screen of the same nature as that which we had seen. Facing it there was assembled an audience of at least a thousand people, who set up a murmur of welcome as we entered. They were of both sexes and of all ages, the men dark and bearded, the women beautiful in youth and dignified in age. We had little time to observe them, for we were led to seats in the front row, and Maracot was then placed on a stand opposite the screen, the lights were in some fashion turned down, and he had the signal to begin.

And excellently well he played his part. We first saw our vessel sailing forth from the Thames, and a buzz of excitement went up from the tense audience at this authentic glimpse of a real modern city. Then a map appeared which marked her course. Then was seen the steel shell with its fittings, which was greeted with a murmur of recognition. We saw ourselves once more descending, and reaching the edge of the abyss. Then came the appearance of the monster who had wrecked us. "Marax! Marax!" cried the people, as the beast appeared. It was clear that they had learned to know and to fear it. There was a terrified hush as the creature fumbled with our hawser, and a groan of horror as the wires parted and we dropped into the gulf. In a month of explanation we could not have made our plight so clear as in that half-hour of visible demonstration.

As the audience broke up they showered every sign of sympathy upon us, crowding round us and patting our backs to show that we were welcome. We were presented in turn to some of the chiefs, but the chieftainship seemed to lie in wisdom alone, for all appeared to be on the same social scale, and were dressed in much the same way. The men wore tunics of a saffron colour coming down to the knees, with belts and high boots of a scaly tough material which must have been the hide of some sea beast. The women were beautifully draped in classical style, their flowing robes of every tint of pink and blue and green, ornamented with clusters of pearl or opalescent sheets of shell. Many of them were lovely beyond any earthly comparison. There was one—but why should I mix my private feelings up with this public narrative? Let me say only that Mona is the only daughter of Scarpa, one of the leaders of the people, and that from that first day of meeting I read in her dark eyes a message of sympathy and of understanding which went home to my heart, as my gratitude and admiration may have gone to hers. I need not say more at present about this exquisite lady. Suffice it that a new and strong influence had come into my life. When I saw Maracot gesticulating with unwonted animation to one kindly lady, while Scanlan stood conveying his admiration in pantomime in the centre of a group of laughing girls, I realized that my companions also had begun to find that there was a lighter side to our tragic position. If we were dead to the world we had at least found a life beyond, which promised some compensation for what we had lost.

Later in the day we were guided by Manda and other friends round some portions of the immense building. It had been so embedded in the sea-floor by the accumulations of ages that it was only through the roof that it could be entered, and from this point the passages led down and down until the floor level was reached several hundred feet below the entrance chamber. The floor in turn had been excavated, and we saw in all directions passages which sloped downwards into the bowels of the earth. We were shown the air-making apparatus with the pumps which circulated it through the building. Maracot pointed out with wonder and admiration that not only was the oxygen united with the nitrogen, but that smaller retorts supplied other gases which could only be the argon, neon, and other little-known constituents of the atmosphere which we are only just beginning to understand. The distilling vats for making fresh water and the enormous electrical instalments were other objects of interest, but much of the machinery was so intricate that it was difficult for us to follow the details. I can only say that I saw with my own eyes, and tested with my own palate, that chemicals in gaseous and liquid forms were poured into various machines, that they were treated by heat, by pressure, and by electricity, and that flour, tea, coffee, or wine was collected as the product.

There was one consideration which was very quickly forced upon us by our examination, on various occasions, of as much of this building as was open to our inspection. This was that the exposure to the sea had been foreseen and the protection against the inrush of the water had been prepared long before the land sank beneath the waves. Of course, it stood to reason, and needed no proof, that such precautions could not have been taken after the event, but we were witnesses now of the signs that the whole great building had from the first been constructed with the one idea of being an enduring ark of refuge. The huge retorts and vats in which the air, the food, the distilled water, and the other necessary products were made were all built into the walls, and were evidently integral parts of the original construction. So, too, with the exit chambers, the silica works where the vitrine bells were constructed, and the huge pumps which controlled the water. Every one of these things had been prepared by the skill and the foresight of that wonderful far-away people who seemed, from what we could learn, to have thrown out one arm to Central America and one to Egypt, and so left traces of themselves even upon this earth when their own land went down into the Atlantic. As to these, their descendants, we judged that they had probably degenerated, as was but natural, and that at the most they had been stagnant and only preserved some of the science and knowledge of their ancestors without having the energy to add to it. They possessed wonderful powers and yet seemed to us to be strangely wanting in initiative, and had added nothing to that wonderful legacy which they had inherited. I am sure that Maracot, using this knowledge, would very soon have attained greater results. As to Scanlan, with his quick brain and mechanical skill, he was continually putting in touches which probably seemed as remarkable to them as their powers to us. He had a beloved mouth-organ in his coat-pocket when we made our descent, and his use of this was a perpetual joy to our companions, who sat around in entranced groups as we might listen to a Mozart, while he handed out to them the crooning coon songs of his native land.

I have said that the whole building was not open to our inspection, and I might give a little further detail upon that subject. There was one well-worn corridor down which we saw folk continually passing, but which was always avoided by our guides in our excursions. As was natural our curiosity was aroused, and we determined one evening that we would take a chance and do a little exploring upon our own account. We slipped out of our room, therefore, and made our way to the unknown quarter at a time when few people were about.

The passage led us to a high arched door, which appeared to be made of solid gold. When we pushed it open we found ourselves in a huge room, forming a square of not less than two hundred feet. All around the walls were painted with vivid colours and adorned with extraordinary pictures and statues of grotesque creatures with enormous headdresses, like the full-dress regalia of our American Indians. At the end of this great hall there was one huge seated figure, the legs crossed like a Buddha, but with none of the benignity of aspect which is seen on the Buddha's placid features. On the contrary, this was a creature of wrath, open-mouthed and fierce-eyed; the latter being red, and their effect exaggerated by two electric lights which shone through them. On his lap was a great oven, which we observed, as we approached it, to be filled with ashes.

"Moloch!" said Maracot. "Moloch or Baal—the old god of the Phoenician races."

"Good heavens!" I cried, with recollections of old Carthage before me. "Don't tell me that these gentle folk could go in for human sacrifice."

"Look it here, Bo!" said Scanlan anxiously. "I hope they keep it in the family, anyhow. We don't want them to pull no such dope on us."

"No, I guess they have learned their lesson," said I. "It's misfortune that teaches folk to have pity for others."

"That's right," Maracot remarked, poking about among the ashes, "it is the old hereditary god, but it is surely a gentler cult. These are burned loaves and the like. But perhaps there was a time——"

But our speculations were interrupted by a stern voice at our elbow, and we found several men in yellow garments and high hats, who were clearly the priests of the Temple. From the expression on their faces I should judge that we were very near to being the last victims to Baal, and one of them had actually drawn a knife from his girdle. With fierce gestures and cries they drove us roughly out of their sacred shrine.

"By gosh!" cried Scanlan. "I'll sock that duck if he keeps crowding me! Look it here, you Bindlestiff, keep your hands off my coat."

For a moment I feared that we should have had what Scanlan called a "rough house" within the sacred precincts. However, we got the angry mechanic away without blows and regained the shelter of our room, but we could tell from the demeanour of Manda and others of our friends that our escapade was known and resented.

But there was another shrine which was freely

shown to us and which had a very unexpected result, for it opened up a slow and imperfect method of communication between our companions and ourselves. This was a room in the lower quarter of the Temple, with no decorations or distinction save that at one end there stood a statue of ivory yellow with age, representing a woman holding a spear with an owl perched upon her shoulder. A very old man was the guardian of the room, and in spite of his age it was clear to us that he was of a very different race, and one of a finer, larger type than the men of the Temple. As we stood gazing at the ivory statue, Maracot and I, both wondering where we had seen something like it, the old man addressed us.

"Thea" said he, pointing to the figure.

"By George!" I cried. "He is speaking Greek.

"Thea! Athena!" repeated the man.

There was not a doubt of it. "Goddess—Athena," the words were unmistakable. Maracot, whose wonderful brain had absorbed something from every branch of human knowledge, began at once to ask questions in classical Greek which were only partly understood and were answered in a dialect so archaic that it was almost incomprehensible. Still, he acquired some knowledge, and he found an intermediary through whom he could dimly convey something to our companions.

"It is remarkable proof," said Maracot that evening, in his high neighing voice and in the tones of one addressing a large class, "of the reliability of legend. There is always a basis of fact even if in the course of the years it should become distorted. You are aware—or probably you are not aware"—("Bet your life!" from Scanlan)—"that a war was going on between the primitive Greeks and the Atlanteans at the time of the destruction of the great island. The fact is recorded in Solon's description of what he learned from the priests of Sais. We may conjecture that there were Greek prisoners in the hands of the Atlanteans at the time, that some of them were in the service of the Temple, and that they carried their own religion with them. That man was, so far as I could understand, the old hereditary priest of the cult, and perhaps when we know more we shall see something of these ancient people."

"Well, I hand it to them for good sense," said Scanlan. "I guess if you want a plaster god it is better to have a fine woman than that blatherskite with the red eyes and the coal-bunker on his knees."

"Lucky they can't understand your views," I remarked. "If they did you might end up as a Christian martyr."

"Not so long as I can play them jazz," he answered. "I guess they've got used to me now, and they couldn't do without me."

They were a cheerful crowd, and it was a happy life, but there were and are times when one's whole heart goes out to the homelands which we have lost, and visions of the dear old quadrangles of Oxford, or of the ancient elms and the familiar campus of Harvard, came up before my mind. In those early days they seemed as far from me as some landscape in the moon, and only now in a dim uncertain fashion does the hope of seeing them once more begin to grow in my soul.

CHAPTER IV

It was a few days after our arrival that our hosts or our captors—we were dubious sometimes as to which to call them—took us out for an expedition upon the bottom of the ocean. Six of them came with us, including Manda, the chief. We assembled in the same exit chamber in which we had originally been received, and we were now in a condition to examine it a little more closely. It was a very large place, at least a hundred feet each way, and its low walls and ceiling were green with marine growths and dripping with moisture. A long row of pegs, with marks which I presume were numbers, ran round the whole room, and on each was hung one of the semi-transparent bells of vitrine and a pair of the shoulder batteries which ensured respiration. The floor was of flagged stone worn into concavities, the footsteps of many generations, these hollows now lying as pools of shallow water. The whole was highly illuminated by fluor tubes round the cornice. We were fastened into our vitrine coverings, and a stout pointed staff made of some light metal was handed to each of us. Then, by signals, Manda ordered us to take a grip of a rail which ran round the room, he and his friends setting us an example. The object of this soon became evident, for as the outer door swung slowly open the sea water came pouring in with such force that we should have been swept from our feet but for this precaution. It rose rapidly, however, to above the level of our heads, and the pressure upon us was eased. Manda led the way to the door, and an instant afterwards we were out on the ocean bed once more, leaving the portal open behind us ready for our return.

Looking round us in the cold, flickering, spectral light which illuminates the bathybian plain, we could see for a radius of at least a quarter of a mile in every direction. What amazed us was to observe, on the very limit of what was visible, a very brilliant glow of radiance. It was towards this that our leader turned his steps, our party walking in single file behind him. It was slow going, for there was the resistance of the water, and our feet were buried deeply in the soft slush with every step; but soon we were able to see clearly what the beacon was which had attracted us. It was our own shell, our last reminder of terrestrial life, which lay tilted upon one of the cupolas of the far-flung building, with all its lights still blazing. It was three quarters full of water, but the imprisoned air still preserved that portion in which our electric instalment lay. It was strange indeed as we gazed into it to see the familiar interior with our settees and instruments still in position, while several good-sized fish like minnows in a bottle swam round and round inside it. One after the other our party clambered in through the open flap, Maracot to rescue a book of notes which floated on the surface, Scanlan and I to pick up some personal belongings. Manda came also with one or two of his comrades, examining with the greatest interest the bathymeter and thermometer with the other instruments which were attached to the wall. The latter we detached and took away with us. It may interest scientists to know that forty degrees Fahrenheit represents the temperature at the greatest sea depth to which man has ever descended, and that it is higher, on account of the chemical decomposition of the ooze, than the upper strata of the sea.

Our little expedition had, it seems, a definite object besides that of allowing us a little exercise upon the bed of the ocean. We were hunting for food. Every now and then I saw our comrades strike sharply down with their pointed sticks, impaling each time a large brown flat fish, not unlike a turbot, which was numerous, but lay so closely in the ooze that it took practised eyes to detect it. Soon each of the little men had two or three of these dangling at their sides. Scanlan and I soon got the knack of it, and captured a couple each, but Maracot walked as one in a dream, quite lost in his wonder at the ocean beauties around him and making long and excited speeches which were lost to the ear, but visible to the eyes from the contortion of his features.

Our first impression had been one of monotony, but we soon found that the gray plains were broken up into varied formations by the action of the deep-sea currents which flowed like submarine rivers across them. These streams cut channels in the soft slime and exposed the beds which lay beneath. The floor of these banks consisted of the red clay which forms the base of all things on the surface of the bed of the ocean, and they were thickly studded with white objects which I imagined to be shells, but which proved, when we examined them, to be the ear bones of whales and the teeth of sharks and other sea monsters. One of these teeth which I picked up was fifteen inches long, and we could but be thankful that so fearful a monster frequented the higher levels of ocean. It belonged, according to Maracot, to a giant killing grampus or Orca gladiator. It recalled the observation of Mitchell Hedges that even the most terrible sharks that he had caught bore upon their bodies the marks which showed that they had encountered creatures larger and more formidable than themselves.

There was one peculiarity of the ocean depths which impresses itself upon the observer. There is, as I have said, a constant cold light rising up from the slow phosphorescent decay of the great masses of organic matter. But above, all is black as night. The effect is that of a dim winter day, with a heavy black thundercloud lying low above the earth. Out of this black canopy there falls slowly an incessant snowstorm of tiny white flakes, which glimmer against the sombre background. These are the shells of sea snails and other small creatures who live and die in the five miles of water which separate us from the surface, and though many of these are dissolved as they fall and add to the lime salts in the ocean, the rest go in the course of ages to form that deposit which had entombed the great city in the upper part of which we now dwelt.

Leaving our last link with earth beneath us, we pushed on into the gloom of the submarine world and soon we were met by a completely new development. A moving patch appeared in front of us, which broke up as we approached it into a crowd of men, each in his vitrine envelope, who were dragging behind them broad sledges heaped with coal. It was heavy work, and the poor devils were bending and straining, tugging hard at the shark-skin ropes which served as traces. With each gang of men there was one who appeared to be in authority, and it interested us to see that the leaders and the workers were clearly of a different race. The latter were tall men, fair, with blue eyes and powerful bodies. The others were, as already described, dark and almost negroid, with squat, broad frames. We could not inquire into the mystery at that moment, but the impression was left upon my mind that the one race represented the hereditary slaves of the other, and Maracot was of opinion that they may have been the descendants of those Greek prisoners whose goddess we had seen in the Temple.

Several droves of these men, each drawing its loads of coal, were met by us before we came to the mine itself. At this point the deep-sea deposits and the sandy formations which lay beneath them had been cut away, and a great pit exposed, which consisted of alternate layers of clay and coal, representing strata in the old perished world of long ago which now lay at the bottom of the Atlantic. At the various levels of this huge excavation we could see gangs of men at work hewing the coal, while others gathered it into loads and placed it in baskets, by means of which it was hoisted up to the level above. The whole mine was on so vast a scale that we could not see the other side of the enormous pit which so many generations of workers had scooped in the bed of the ocean. This, then, transmuted into electric force, was the source of the motive power by which the whole machinery of Atlantis was run. It is interesting, by the way, to record that the name of the old city had been correctly preserved in the legends, for when we had mentioned it to Manda and others they first looked greatly surprised that we should know it, and then nodded their heads vigorously to show that they understood.

Passing the great coal pit—or, rather, branching away from it to the right—we came on a line of low cliffs of basalt, their surface as clear and shining as on the day when they were shot up from the bowels of the earth, while their summit, some hundreds of feet above us, loomed up against the dark background.

The base of these volcanic cliffs was draped in a deep jungle of high seaweed, flowing out of tangled masses of crinoid corals laid down in the old terrestrial days. Along the edge of this thick undergrowth we wandered for some time, our companions beating it with their sticks and driving out for our amusement an extraordinary assortment of strange fishes and crustacea, now and again securing a specimen for their own tables. For a mile or more we wandered along in this happy fashion, when I saw Manda stop suddenly and look round him with gestures of alarm and surprise. These submarine gestures formed a language in themselves, for in a moment his companions understood the cause of his trouble, and then with a shock we realized it also. Dr. Maracot had disappeared.

He had certainly been with us at the coal pit, and he had come as far as the basalt cliffs. It was inconceivable that he had got ahead of us, so it was evident that he must be somewhere along the line of jungle in our rear. Though our friends were disturbed, Scanlan and I who knew something of the good man's absentminded eccentricities, were confident that there was no cause for alarm, and that we should soon find him loitering over some sea form which had attracted him. We all turned to retrace our steps, and had hardly gone a hundred yards before we caught sight of him.

But he was running—running with an agility which I should have thought impossible for a man of his habits. Even the least athletic can run, however, when fear is the pace-maker. His hands were outstretched for help, and he stumbled and blundered forward with clumsy energy. He had good cause to exert himself, for three horrible creatures were close at his heels. They were tiger crabs, striped black and white, each about the size of a Newfoundland dog. Fortunately they were themselves not very swift travellers, and were scurrying along the soft sea bottom in a curious side-long fashion which was little faster than that of the terrified fugitive.

Their wind was better, however, and they would probably have had their horrible claws upon him in a very few minutes had not our friends intervened. They dashed forward with their pointed sticks, and Manda flashed a powerful electric lantern, which he carried in his belt, in the faces of the loathsome monsters, who scuttled into the jungle and were lost to view. Our comrade sat down on a lump of coral and his face showed that he was exhausted by his adventure. He told us afterwards that he had penetrated the jungle in the hope of securing what seemed to him to be a rare specimen of the deep-sea Chimoera, and that he had blundered into the nest of these fierce tiger crabs, who had instantly dashed after him. It was only after a long rest that he was able to resume the journey.

Our next stage after skirting the basalt cliffs led us to our goal. The gray plain in front of us was covered at this point by irregular hummocks and tall projections, which told us that the great city of old lay beneath it. It would all have been completely buried forever by the ooze, as Herculaneum has been by lava or Pompeii by ashes, had an entrance to it not been excavated by the survivors of the Temple. This entrance was a long, downward cutting, which ended up in a broad street with buildings exposed on either side. The walls of these buildings were occasionally cracked and shattered, for they were not of the solid construction which had preserved the temple, but the interiors were in most cases exactly as they had been when the catastrophe occurred, save the sea changes of all sorts, beautiful and rare in some cases and horrifying in others, had modified the appearances of the rooms. Our guides did not encourage us to examine the first ones which we reached, but hurried us onward until we came to that which had clearly been the great central citadel or palace round which the whole town centred. The pillars and columns and vast sculptured cornices and friezes and staircases of this building exceeded anything which I have ever seen upon earth. Its nearest approach seemed to me to be the remains of the Temple of Karnak at Luxor in Egypt, and, strange to say, the decorations and half-effaced engravings resembled in detail those of the great ruin beside the Nile, and the lotus-shaped capitals of the columns were the same. It was an amazing experience to stand in the marble tessellated floors of those vast halls, with great statues looming high above one on every side, and to see, as we saw that day, huge silvery eels gliding above our heads and frightened fish darting away in every direction from the light which was projected before us. From room to room we wandered, marking every sign of luxury and occasionally of that lascivious folly which is said, by the lingering legend, to have drawn God's curse upon the people. One small room was wonderfully enamelled with mother-of-pearl, so that even now it gleamed with brilliant opalescent tints when the light played across it. An ornamented platform of yellow metal and a similar couch lay in one corner, and one felt that it may well have been the bedchamber of a queen, but beside the couch there lay now a loathsome black squid, its foul body rising and falling in a slow, stealthy rhythm so that it seemed like some evil heart which still beat in the very centre of the wicked palace. I was glad, and so, I learned, were my companions, when our guides led the way out once more, glancing for a moment at a ruined amphitheatre and again at a pier with a lighthouse at the end, which showed that the city had been a seaport. Soon we had emerged from these places of ill omen and were out in the familiar bathybian plain once more.

Our adventures were not quite over, for there was one more which was as alarming to our companions as to ourselves. We had nearly made our way home when one of our guides pointed upward with alarm. Gazing in that direction we saw an extraordinary sight. Out of the black gloom of the waters a huge, dark figure was emerging, falling rapidly downwards. At first it seemed a shapeless mass, but as it came more clearly into the light we could see that it was the dead body of a monstrous fish, which had burst so that the entrails were streaming up behind it as it fell. No doubt the gases had buoyed it up in the higher reaches of the ocean until, having been released by putrefaction or by the ravages of sharks, there was nothing left but dead weight, which sent it hurtling down to the bottom of the sea. Already in our walk we had observed several of these great skeletons picked clean by the fish, but this creature was still, save for its disembowelment, even as it had lived. Our guides seized us with the intention of dragging us out of the path of the falling mass, but presently they were reassured and stood still, for it was clear that it would miss us. Our vitrine helmets prevented our hearing the thud, but it must have been prodigious when that huge body struck the floor of the ocean, and we saw the Globigerina ooze fly upwards as the mud splashes when a heavy stone is hurled into it. It was a sperm whale, some seventy feet long, and from the excited and joyful gestures of the submarine folk I gathered that they would find plenty of use for the spermaceti and the fat. For the moment, however, we left the derelict creature, and with joyful hearts, for we unpractised visitors were weary and aching, found ourselves once more in front of the engraved portal of the roof, and finally standing safe and sound, divested of our vitrine bells, on the sloppy floor of the entrance chamber.

A few days—as we reckon time—after the occasion when we had given the community a cinema view of our own proceedings, we were present at a very much more solemn and august exhibition of the same sort, which gave us in a clear and wonderful way the past history of this remarkable people. I cannot flatter myself that it was given entirely on our behalf, for I rather think that the events were publicly rehearsed from time to time in order to carry on the record, and that the part to which we were admitted was only some intermezzo of a long religious ceremony. However that may be, I will describe it exactly as it occurred.

We were led to the same great hall or theatre where Dr. Maracot had thrown our own adventures upon the screen. There the whole community was assembled, and we were given, as before, places of honour in front of the great luminous screen. Then, after a long song, which may have been some sort of patriotic chant, a very old white-haired man, the historian or chronicler of the nation, advanced amid much applause to the focus point and threw upon the bright surface before him a series of pictures to represent the rise and fall of his own people. I wish I could convey to you their vividness and drama. My two companions and I lost all sense of time and place, so absorbed were we in the contemplation, while the audience was moved to its depths, and groaned or wept as the tragedy unfolded, which depicted the ruin of their fatherland, the destruction of their race.

In the first series of scenes we saw the old continent in its glory, as its memory had been handed down by these historical records passed from fathers to sons. We had a bird's-eye view of a glorious rolling country, enormous in extent, well watered and cleverly irrigated, with great fields of grain, waving orchards, lovely streams and woody hills, still lakes and occasional picturesque mountains. It was studded with villages and covered with farmhouses and beautiful private residences. Then our attention was carried to the capital, a wonderful and gorgeous city upon the seashore, the harbour crammed with galleys, her quays piled with merchandise, and her safety assured by high walls with towering battlements and circular moats, all on the most gigantic scale. The houses stretched inland for many miles, and in the centre of the city was a crenellated castle or citadel, so widespread and commanding that it was like some creation of a dream. We were then shown the faces of those who lived in that golden age, wise and venerable old men, virile warriors, saintly priests, beautiful and dignified women, lovely children, an apotheosis of the human race.

Then came pictures of another sort. We saw wars, constant wars, war by land and war by sea. We saw naked and defenceless races trampled down and overridden by great chariots or the rush of mailed horsemen. We saw treasures heaped upon the victors, but even as the riches increased the faces upon the screen became more animal and more cruel. Down, down they sank from one generation to another. We were shown signs of lascivious dissipation or moral degeneracy, of the accretion of matter and decline of spirit. Brutal sports at the expense of others had taken the place of the manly exercises of old. There was no longer the quiet and simple family life, nor the cultivation of the mind, but we had a glimpse of a people who were restless and shallow, rushing from one pursuit to another, grasping ever at pleasure, forever missing it, and yet imagining always that in some more complex and unnatural form it might still be found. There had arisen on the one hand an over-rich class who sought only sensual gratification, and on the other hand an over-poor residue whose whole function in life was to minister to the wants of their masters, however evil those wants might be.

And now once again a new note was struck. There were reformers at work who were trying to turn the nation from its evil ways, and to direct it back into those higher paths which it had forsaken. We saw them, grave and earnest men, reasoning and pleading with the people, but we saw them scorned and jeered at by those whom they were trying to save. Especially we could see that it was the priests of Baal, priests who had gradually allowed forms and show and outward ceremonies to take the place of unselfish spiritual development, who led the opposition to the reformers. But the latter were not to be bullied or brow-beaten. They continued to try for the salvation of the people, and their faces assumed a graver and even a terror-inspiring aspect, as those of men who had a fearsome warning to give which was like some dreadful vision before their own minds. Of their auditors some few seemed to heed and be terrified at the words, but others turned away laughing and plunged ever deeper into their morass of sin. There came a time at last when the reformers turned away also as men who could do no more, and left this degenerate people to its fate.

Then we saw a strange sight. There was one reformer, a man of singular strength of mind and body, who gave a lead to all the others. He had wealth and influence and powers, which latter seemed to be not entirely of this earth. We saw him in what seemed to be a trance, communing with higher spirits. It was he who brought all the science of his land—science which far outshone anything known by us moderns—to the task of building an ark of refuge against the coming troubles. We saw myriads of workmen at work, and the walls rising while crowds of careless citizens looked on and made merry at such elaborate and useless precautions. We saw others who seemed to reason with him and to say to him that if he had fears it would be easier for him to fly to some safer land. His answer, so far as we could follow it, was that there were some who must be saved at the last moment, and that for their sake he must remain in the new Temple of safety. Meanwhile, he collected in it those who had followed him, and he held them there, for he did not himself know the day nor the hour, though forces beyond mortal had assured him of the coming fact. So when the ark was ready and the water-tight doors were finished and tested, he waited upon doom, with his family, his friends, his followers, and his servants.

And doom came. It was a terrible thing even in a picture. God knows what it could be like in reality. We first saw a huge sleek mountain of water rise to an incredible height out of a calm ocean. Then we saw it travel, sweeping on and on, mile after mile, a great glistening hill, topped with foam, at an ever-increasing rate. Two little chips tossing among the snowy fringe upon the summit became, as the wave rolled towards us, a couple of shattered galleys. Then we saw it strike the shore and sweep over the city, while the houses went down before it like a field of corn before a tornado. We saw the folk upon the house-tops glaring out at the approaching death, their faces twisted with horror, their eyes staring, their mouths contorted, gnawing at their hands and gibbering in an insanity of terror. The very men and women who had mocked at the warning were now screaming to heaven for mercy, grovelling with their faces on the ground, or kneeling with frenzied arms raised in wild appeal. There was no time now to reach the ark, which stood beyond the city, but thousands dashed up to the Citadel, which stood upon higher ground, and the battlement walls were black with people. Then suddenly the Castle began to sink. Everything began to sink. The water had poured down into the remote recesses of the earth, the central fires had expanded it into steam, and the very foundations of the land were blown apart. Down went the city and ever down, while a cry went up from ourselves and the audience at the terrible sight. The pier broke in two and vanished. The high Pharus collapsed under the waves. The roofs looked for a while like successive reefs of rock forming lines of spouting breakers until they, too, went under. The Citadel was left alone upon the surface, like some monstrous ship, and then it also slid sideways down into the abyss, with a fringe of helpless waving hands upon its summit. The awful drama was over, and an unbroken sea lay across the whole continent, a sea which bore no life upon it, but which among its huge smoking swirls and eddies showed all the wrack of the tragedy tossed hither and thither, dead men and animals, chairs, tables, articles of clothing, floating hats and bales of goods, all bobbing and heaving in one huge liquid fermentation. Slowly we saw it die away, and a great wide expanse as smooth and bright as quicksilver, with a murky sun low on the horizon, showed us the grave of the land that God had weighed and found wanting.

The story was complete. We could ask for no more, since our own brains and imagination could supply the rest. We realized the slow, remorseless descent of that great land lower and lower into the abyss of the ocean amid volcanic convulsions which threw up submarine peaks around it. We saw it in our mind's eye stretched out, over miles of what was now the bed of the Atlantic, the shattered city lying alongside of the ark of refuge in which the handful of nerve-shattered survivors were assembled. And then finally we understood how these had carried on their lives, how they used the various devices with which the foresight and science of their great leader had endowed them, how he had taught them all his arts before he passed away, and how some fifty or sixty survivors had grown now into a large community, which had to dig its way into the bowels of the earth in order to get room to expand. No library of information could make it clearer than that series of pictures and the inferences which we could draw from them. Such was the fate, and such the causes of the fate, which overwhelmed the great land of Atlantis. Some day far distant, when this bathybian ooze has turned to chalk, this great city will be thrown up once more by some fresh expiration of Nature, and the geologist of the future, delving in the quarry, will exhume not flints nor shells, but the remains of a vanished civilization and the traces of an old-world catastrophe.

Only one point had remained undecided, and that was the length of time since the tragedy had occurred. Dr. Maracot discovered a rough method of making an estimate. Among the many annexes of the great building there was one huge vault, which was the burial place of the chiefs. As in Egypt and in Yucatan, the practise of mummifying had been usual, and in niches in the walls there were endless rows of these grim relics of the past. Manda pointed proudly to the next one in the succession, and gave us to understand that it was specially arranged for himself.

"If you take an average of the European kings," said Maracot, in his best professorial manner, "you will find that they run to about five in the century. We may adopt the same figure here. We cannot hope for scientific accuracy, but it will give us an approximation. I have counted the mummies, and they are four hundred in number."

"Then it would be eight thousand years?"

"Exactly. And this agrees to some extent with Plato's estimate. It certainly occurred before the Egyptian written records begin, and they go back between six and seven thousand years from the present date. Yes, I think we may say that our eyes have seen the reproduction of a tragedy which occurred at least eight thousand years ago. But, of course, to build up such a civilization as we see the traces of must in itself have taken many thousands of years.

"Thus," he concluded—and I pass the claim on to you—"we have extended the horizon of ascertained human history as no men have ever done since history began."

CHAPTER V

It was about a month, according to our calculations, after our visit to the buried city that the most amazing and unexpected thing of all occurred. We had thought by this time that we were immune to shocks and that nothing new could really stagger us, but this actual fact went far beyond anything for which our imagination might have prepared us.

It was Scanlan who brought the news that something momentous had happened. You must realize that by this time we were, to some extent, at home in the great building; that we knew where the common rest rooms and recreation rooms were situated; that we attended concerts (their music was very strange and elaborate) and theatrical entertainments, where the unintelligible words were translated by very vivid and dramatic gestures; and that, speaking generally, we were part of the community. We visited various families in their own private rooms, and our lives—I can speak for my own, at any rate—were made the brighter by the glamour of these strange people, especially of that one dear young lady whose name I have already mentioned. Mona was the daughter of one of the leaders of the tribe, and I found in his family a warm and kindly welcome which rose above all differences of race or language. When it comes to the most tender language of all, I did not find that there was so much between old Atlantis and modern America. I guess that what would please a Massachusetts girl of Brown's College is just about what would please my lady under the waves.

But I must get back to the fact that Scanlan came into our room with news of some great happening.

"Say, there is one of them just blown in, and he's that excited that he clean forgot to take his glass lid off, and he was jabbering for some minutes before he understood that no one could hear him. Then it was Blah Blah Blah as long as his breath would hold, and they are all following him now to the jumping-off place. It's me for the water, for there is sure something worth our seeing."

Running out, we found our friends all hurrying down the corridor with excited gestures, and we, joining the procession, soon formed part of the crowd who were hurrying across the sea bottom, led by the excited messenger. They drove along at a rate which made it no easy matter for us to keep up, but they carried their electric lanterns with them, and even though we fell behind we were able to follow the gleam. The route lay as before, along the base of the basalt cliffs until we came to a spot where a set of steps, concave from long usage, led up to the top. Ascending these, we found ourselves in broken country, with many jagged pinnacles of rock and deep crevasses which made it difficult travelling. Emerging from this tangle of ancient lava, we came out on a circular plain, brilliant in the phosphorescent light, and there in the very centre of it lay an object which set me gasping. As I looked at my companions I could see from their amazed expression how fully they shared my emotion.

Half embedded in the slime there lay a good-sized steamer. It was tilted upon its side, the funnel had broken and was hanging at a strange angle, and the foremast had snapped short off, but otherwise the vessel was intact and as clean and fresh as if she had just left the dock. We hurried towards her and found ourselves under the stern. You can imagine how we felt when we read the name "*Stratford*, London." Our ship had followed ourselves into the Maracot Deep.

Of course, after the first shock the affair did not seem so incomprehensible. We remembered the falling glass, the reefed sails of the experienced Norwegian skipper, the strange black cloud upon the horizon. Clearly there had been a sudden cyclone of phenomenal severity and the *Stratford* had been blown over. It was too evident that all her people were dead, for most of the boats were trailing in different states of destruction from the davits, and in any case what boat could live in such a hurricane? The tragedy had occurred, no doubt, within an hour or two of our own disaster. Perhaps the sounding-line which we had seen had only just been wound in before the blow fell. It was terrible, but whimsical, that we should be still alive, while those who were mourning our destruction had themselves been destroyed. We had no means of telling whether the ship had drifted in the upper levels of the ocean or whether she had lain for some time where we found her before she was discovered by the Atlantean.

Poor Howie, the captain, or what was left of him, was still at his post upon the bridge, the rail grasped firmly in his stiffened hands. His body and that of three stokers in the engine-room were the only ones which had sunk with the ship. They were each removed under our direction and buried under the ooze with a wreath of sea-flowers over their remains. I give this detail in the hope that it may be some comfort to Mrs. Howie in her bereavement. The names of the stokers were unknown to us.

Whilst we had been performing this duty the little men had swarmed over the ship. Looking up, we saw them everywhere, like mice upon a cheese. Their excitement and curiosity made it clear to us that it was the first modern ship—possibly the first steamer—which had ever come down to them. We found out later that their oxygen apparatus inside their vitrine bells would not allow of a longer absence from the recharging station than a few hours, and so their chances of learning anything of what was on the sea bed were limited to so many miles from their central base. They set to work at once breaking up the wreck and removing all that would be of use to them, a very long process, which is hardly accomplished yet. We were glad also to make our way to our cabins and to get many of those articles of clothing and books which were not ruined beyond redemption.

Among the other things which we rescued from the *Stratford* was the ship's log, which had been written up to the last day by the captain in view of our own catastrophe. It was strange indeed that we should be reading it and that he should be dead. The day's entry ran thus:

Oct. 3. The three brave but foolhardy adventurers have to-day, against my will and advice, descended in their apparatus to the bottom of the ocean, and the accident which I had foreseen has occurred. God rest their souls. They went down at eleven A.M. and I had some doubts about permitting them, as a squall seemed to be coming up. I would that I had acted upon my impulse, but it would only have postponed the inevitable tragedy. I bade each of them farewell with the conviction that I would see them no more. For a time all was well, and at eleven-forty-five they had reached a depth of three hundred fathoms, where they had found bottom. Dr. Maracot sent several messages to me and all seemed to be in order, when suddenly I heard his voice in agitation, and there was considerable agitation of the wire hawser. An instant later it snapped. It would appear that they were by this time over a deep chasm, for at the Doctor's request the ship had steamed very slowly forward. The air tubes continued to run out for a distance which I should estimate at half a mile, and then they also snapped. It is the last which we can ever hope to hear of Dr. Maracot, Mr. Headley, or Mr. Scanlan.

And yet a most extraordinary thing must be recorded, the meaning of which I have not had time to weigh, for with this foul weather coming up there is much to distract me. A deep-sea sounding was taken at the same time, and the depth recorded was twenty-six thousand six hundred feet. The weight was, of course, left at the bottom, but the wire has just been drawn in and, incredible as it may seem, above the porcelain sample cup there was found Mr. Headley's handkerchief with his name marked upon it. The ship's company are all amazed, and no one can suggest how such a thing could have occurred. In my next entry I may have more to say about this. We have lingered a few hours in the hope of something coming to the surface, and we have pulled up the hawser, which shows a jagged end. Now I must look to the ship, for I have never seen a worse sky and the barometer is at 28.5 and sinking fast.

So it was that we got the final news of our former companions. A terrific cyclone must have struck her and destroyed her immediately afterwards.

We stayed at the wreck until a certain stuffiness within our vitrine bells and a feeling of increasing weight upon our chests warned us that it was high time to begin our return. Then it was, on our homeward journey, that we had an adventure which showed us the sudden dangers to which these submarine folk are exposed, and which may explain why their numbers, in spite of the lapse of time, were not greater than they were. Including the Grecian slaves we cannot reckon those numbers at more than four or five thousand at the most. We had descended the staircase and were making our way along the edge of the jungle which skirts the basalt cliffs, when Manda pointed excitedly upwards and beckoned furiously to one of our party who was some distance out in the open. At the same time he and those around him ran to the side of some high boulders, pulling us along with them. It was only when we were in their shelter that we saw the cause of the alarm. Some distance above us, but descending rapidly, was a huge fish of a most peculiar shape. It might have been a great floating feather bed, soft and bulging, with a white under-surface and a long red fringe, the vibration of which propelled it through the water. It appeared to have neither mouth nor eyes, but it soon showed that it was formidably alert. The member of our party who was out in the open ran for the same shelter that we had taken, but he was too late. I saw his face convulsed with terror as he realized his fate. The horrible creature descended upon him, enveloped him on all sides, and lay upon him, pulsing in a dreadful way as if it were thrusting his body against the coral rocks and grinding it to pieces. The tragedy was taking place within a few yards of us, and yet our companions were so overcome by the suddenness of it that they seemed to be bereft of all power of action. It was Scanlan who rushed out and, jumping on the creature's broad back, blotched with red and brown markings, dug the sharp end of his metal staff into its soft tissues.

I had followed Scanlan's example and finally Maracot and all of them attacked the monster, which glided slowly off, leaving a trail of oily and glutinous excretion behind it. Our help had come too late, however, for the impact of the great fish had broken the vitrine bell of the Atlantean and he had been drowned. It was a day of mourning when we carried his body back into the Refuge, but it was also a day of triumph for us, for our prompt action had raised us greatly in the estimation of our companions. As to the strange fish, we had Dr. Maracot's assurance that it was a specimen of the blanket fish, well known to ichthyologists, but of a size such as had never entered into his dreams.

I speak of this creature because it chanced to bring about a tragedy, but I could, and perhaps will, write a book upon the wonderful life which we have seen here. Red and black are the prevailing colours in deep-sea life, while the vegetation is of the palest olive, and is of so tough a fibre that it is seldom dragged up by our trawls, so that Science has come to believe that the bed of the ocean is bare. Many of the marine forms are of surprising loveliness, and others so grotesque in their horror that they are like the images of delirium and of a danger such as no land animal can rival. I have seen a black stingray thirty feet long with a horrible fang upon its tail, one blow of which would kill any living creature. I have seen, too, a frog-like beast with protruding green eyes, which is simply a gaping mouth with a huge stomach behind it. To meet it is death unless one has an electric flash with which to repel it. I have seen the blind red eel which lies among the rocks and kills by the emission of poison, and I have seen also the giant sea-scorpion, one of the terrors of the deep, and the hag fish, which lurks among the sea jungle.

Once, too, it was my privilege to see the real sea-serpent, a creature which has seldom appeared before the human eye, for it lives in the extreme depths and is seen on the surface only when some submarine convulsion has driven it out of its haunts. Two of them swam, or rather glided, past us one day while Mona and I cowered among the bunches of lamellaria. They were enormous—some ten feet in height and two hundred in length, black above, silver-white below, with a high fringe upon the back, and small eyes no larger than those of an ox. Of these and many other such things an account will be found in the paper of Dr. Maracot, should it ever reach your hands.

Week glided into week in our new life. It had become a very pleasant one, and we were slowly picking up enough of this long-forgotten tongue to enable us to converse a little with our companions. There were endless subjects both for study and for amusement in the Refuge, and already Maracot has mastered so much of the old chemistry that he declares that he can revolutionize all worldly ideas if he can only transmit his knowledge. Among other things they have learned to split the atom, and though the energy released is less than our scientists had anticipated, it is still sufficient to supply them with a great reservoir of power. Their acquaintance with the power and nature of the ether is also far ahead of ours, and indeed that strange translation of thought into pictures, by which we had told them our story and they theirs, was due to an etheric impression translated back into terms of matter.

And yet, in spite of their knowledge, there were points connected with modern scientific developments which had been overlooked by their ancestors.

It was left to Scanlan to demonstrate the fact. For weeks he was in a state of suppressed excitement, bursting with some great secret, and chuckling continually at his own thoughts. We only saw him occasionally during this time, for he was extremely busy and his one friend and confidant was a fat and jovial Atlantean named Berbrix, who was in charge of some of the machinery. Scanlan and Berbrix, though their intercourse was carried on chiefly by signs and mutual back-slapping, had become very close friends, and were now continually closeted together. One evening Scanlan came in radiant.

"Look here, Doc," he said to Maracot. "I've a dope of my own that I want to hand to these folk. They've shown us a thing or two, and I figure that it is up to us to return it. What's the matter with calling them together tomorrow night for a show?"

"Jazz or the Charleston?" I asked.

"Charleston nothing. Wait till you see it. Man, it's the greatest stunt—but there, I won't say a word more. Just this, Bo. I won't let you down, for I've got the goods, and I mean to deliver them."

Accordingly, the community were assembled next evening in the familiar hall. Scanlan and Berbrix were on the platform, beaming with pride. One or other of them touched a button, and then—well, to use Scanlan's own language, "I hand it to him, for he did surprise us some!"

"2L. O. calling," cried a clear voice. "London calling the British Isles. Weather forecast." Then followed the usual sentence about depressions and anticyclones. "First Bulletin. His Majesty the King this morning opened the new wing of the Children's Hospital in Hammersmith——" and so on and on, in the familiar strain. For the first time we were back in a workaday England once more, plodding bravely through its daily task, with its stout back bowed under its war debts. Then we heard the foreign news, the sporting news. The old world was droning on the same as ever. Our friends the Atlanteans listened in amazement, but without comprehension. When, however, as the first item after the news, the Guards' band struck up the march from *Lohengrin* a positive shout of delight broke from the people, and it was funny to see them rush upon the platform, and turn over the curtains, and look behind the screens to find the source of the music. Yes, we have left our mark forever upon the submarine civilization.

"No, sir," said Scanlan afterwards. "I could not make an issuing station. They have not the material, and I have not the brains. But down at home I rigged a two-valve set of my own with the aërial beside the clothes line in the yard, and I learned to handle it, and to pick up any station in the States. It seemed to me funny if, with all this electricity to hand, and with their glasswork ahead of ours, we couldn't vamp up something that would catch an ether wave, and a wave would sure travel through water just as easy as through air. Old Berbrix nearly threw a fit when we got the first call, but he is wise to it now, and I guess it's a permanent institution."

Among the discoveries of the Atlantean chemists is a gas which is nine times lighter than hydrogen and which Maracot has named levigen. It was his experiments with this which gave us the idea of sending glass balls with information as to our fate to the surface of the ocean.

"I have made Manda understand the idea," said he. "He has given orders to the silica workers, and in a day or two the globes will be ready."

"But how can we get our news inside?" I asked.

"There is a small aperture left through which the gas is inserted. Into this we can push the papers. Then these skilful workers can seal up the hole. I am assured that when we release them they will shoot up to the surface."

"And bob about unseen for a year."

"That might be. But the ball would reflect the sun's rays. It would surely attract attention. We were on the line of shipping between Europe and South America. I see no reason why, if we send several, one at least may not be found."

And this, my dear Talbot, or you others who read this narrative, is how it comes into your hands. But a far more fateful scheme may lie behind it. The idea came from the fertile brain of the American mechanic.

"Say, friends," said he, as we sat alone in our chamber, "it's dandy down here, and the drink is good and the eats are good, and I've met a wren that makes anything in Philadelphia look like two cents, but all the same there are times when I want to feel that I might see God's own country once more."

"We may all feel that way," said I, "but I don't see how you can hope to make it."

"Look it here, Bo! these balls of gas could carry up our message, maybe they could carry us up also. Don't think I'm joshing, for I've figured it out to rights. We will suppose we put three or four of them together so as to get a good lift. See? Then we have our vitrine bells on and harness ourselves on to the balls. When the bell rings we cut loose and up we go. What is going to stop us between here and the surface?"

"A shark, maybe."

"Blah! Sharks nothing! We would streak past any shark so's he'd hardly know we was there. He'd think we was three flashes of light and we'd get such a kick on that we'd shoot fifty feet up in the air at the other end. I tell you the goof that sees us come up is going to say his prayers over it."

"But, suppose it is possible, what will happen afterwards?"

"For Pete's sake, leave afterwards out of it! Let us chance our luck, or we are here for keeps. It's me for cutting loose and having a dash at it."

"I certainly greatly desire to return to the world, if only to lay our results before the learned societies," said Maracot. "It is only my personal influence which can make them realize the fund of new knowledge which I have acquired. I should be quite in favour of any such attempt as Scanlan has indicated."

There were good reasons, as I will tell later, which made me the least eager of the three.

"It would be perfect madness as you propose it. Unless we had someone expecting us on the surface we should infallibly drift about and perish from hunger and thirst."

"Shucks, man, how could we have someone expecting us?"

"Perhaps even that could be managed," said Maracot. "We can give within a mile or two the exact latitude and longitude of our position."

"And they would let down a ladder," said I, with some bitterness.

"Ladder nothing! The boss is right. See here, Mr. Headley, you put in that letter that you are going to send the universe—my! don't I see the scare lines in the journals!—that we are at 27 North Latitude and 28.14 West Longitude, or whatever other figure is the right one. Got that? Then you say that three of the most important folk in history, the great man of Science, Maracot, and the rising star bug-collector, Headley, and Bob Scanlan, a peach of a mechanic and the pride of Merribanks, are all yellin' and whoopin' for help from the bottom of the sea. Follow my idee?"

"Well, what then?"

"Well, then it's up to them, you see. It's kind of a challenge that they can't forget. Same as I've read of Stanley finding Livingstone and the like. It's for them to find some way to yank us out or catch us at the other end if we can take the jump ourselves."

"We could suggest the way ourselves," said the Professor. "Let them drop a deep-sea line into these waters and we will look out for it. When it comes we can tie a message to it and bid them stand by for us."

"You've said a mouthful!" cried Bob Scanlan. "That is sure the way to do it."

"And if any lady cared to share our fortunes four would be as easy as three," said Maracot, with a roguish smile at me.

"For that matter, five is as easy as four," said Scanlan. "But you've got it now, Mr. Headley. You write that down, and in six months we shall be back in London River once more."

So now we launch our two balls into that water which is to us what the air is to you. Our two little balloons will go aloft. Will both be lost on the way? It is possible. Or may we hope that one will get through? We leave it on the knees of the gods. If nothing can be done for us, then let those who care for us know that in any case we are safe and happy. If, on the other hand, this suggestion could be carried out and the money and energy for our rescue should be forthcoming, we have given you the means by which it can be done. Meanwhile, good-bye—or is it *au revoir?*

So ended the narrative in the vitrine ball.

The preceding narrative covers the facts so far as they were available when the account was first drawn up. While the script was in the hands of the printer there came an epilogue of the most unexpected and sensational description. I refer to the rescue of the adventurers by Mr. Faverger's steam yacht *Marion* and the account sent out by the wireless transmitter of that vessel, and picked up by the cable station at the Cape de Verde Islands, which has just forwarded it to Europe and America. This account was drawn up by Mr. Key Osborne, the well-known representative of the Associated Press.

It would appear that immediately upon the first narrative of the plight of Dr. Maracot and his friends reaching Europe an expedition was quietly and effectively fitted up in the hope of bringing about a rescue. Mr. Faverger generously placed his famous steam yacht at the disposal of the party, which he accompanied in person. The *Marion* sailed from Cherbourg in June, picked up Mr. Key Osborne and a motion-picture operator at Southampton, and set forth at once for the tract of ocean which was indicated in the original document. This was reached upon the first of July.

A deep-sea piano-wire line was lowered, and was dragged slowly along the bottom of the ocean. At the end of this line, beside the heavy lead, there was suspended a bottle containing a message. The message ran: "Your account has been received by the world, and we are here to help you. We duplicate this message by our wireless transmitter in the hope that it may reach you. We will slowly traverse your region. When you have detached this bottle, please replace your own message in it. We will act upon your instructions."

For two days the *Marion* cruised slowly to and fro without result. On the third a very great surprise awaited the rescue party. A small, highly luminous ball shot out of the water a few hundred yards from the ship, and proved to be a vitreous message-bearer of the sort which had been described in the original document. Having been broken with some difficulty, the following message was read:

Thanks, dear friends. We greatly appreciate your grand loyalty and energy. We receive your wireless messages with facility, and are in a position to answer you in this fashion. We have endeavoured to get possession of your line, but the currents lift it high, and it sweeps along rather faster than even the most active of us can move against the resistance of the water. We propose to make our venture at six to-morrow morning, which should, according to our reckoning, be Tuesday, July 5th. We will come one at a time, so that any advice arising from our experience can be wirelessed back to those who come later. Once again heartfelt thanks.

MARACOT. HEADLEY. SCANLAN.

Mr. Key Osborne now takes up the narrative:

"It was a perfect morning, and the deep sapphire sea lay as smooth as a lake, with the glorious arch of the deep blue sky unbroken by the smallest cloud. The whole crew of the *Marion* was early astir, and awaited events with the most tense interest. As the hour of six drew near our anticipation was painful. A look-out had been placed upon our signal mast, and it was just five minutes to the hour when we heard him shouting, and saw him pointing to the water on our port bow. We all crowded to that side of the deck, and I was able to perch myself on one of the boats from which I had a clear view. I saw through the still water something which looked like a silver bubble ascending with great rapidity from the depths of the ocean. It broke the surface about two hundred yards from the ship, and soared straight up into the air, a beautiful shining globe some three feet in diameter, rising to a great height and then drifting away in some slight current of wind exactly as a toy balloon would do. It was a marvellous sight, but it filled us with apprehension, for it seemed as if the harness might have come loose, and the burden which this tractor should have borne through the waters had been shaken loose upon the way. A wireless was at once dispatched:

" 'Your messenger has appeared close to the vessel. It had nothing attached and has flown away.' Meanwhile we lowered a boat so as to be ready for any development.

"Just after six o'clock there was another signal from our watchman, and an instant later I caught sight of another silver globe, which was swimming up from the depths very much more slowly than the last. On reaching the surface it floated in the air, but its burden was supported upon the water. This burden proved upon examination to be a great bundle of books, papers, and miscellaneous objects all wrapped in a casing of fish skin. It was hoisted dripping upon the deck, and was acknowledged by wireless, while we eagerly awaited the next arrival.

"This was not long in coming. Again the silver bubble, again the breaking of the surface, but this time the glistening ball shot high into the air, suspending under it, to our amazement, the slim figure of a woman. It was but the impetus which had carried her into the air, and an instant later she had been towed to the side of the vessel. A leather circlet had been firmly fastened round the upper curve of the glass ball, and from this long straps depended which were attached to a broad leather belt round her dainty waist. The upper part of her body was covered by a peculiar pear-shaped glass shade—I call it glass, but it was of the same tough light material as the vitreous ball. It was almost transparent, with silvery veins running through its substance. This glass covering had tight elastic attachments at the waist and shoulders, which made it perfectly watertight, while it was provided within, as has been described in Headley's original manuscript, with novel but very light and practical chemical apparatus for the renovation of air. With some difficulty the breathing bell was removed and the lady hoisted upon deck. She lay there in a deep faint, but her regular breathing encouraged us to think that she would soon recover from the effects of her rapid journey and from the change of pressure, which had been minimized by the fact that the density of the air inside the protective sheath was considerably higher than our atmosphere, so that it may be said to have represented that halfway point which human divers are wont to pause. Presumably this is the Atlantean woman referred to in the first message as Mona, and if we may take her as a sample they are indeed a race worth reintroducing to earth. She is dark in complexion, beautifully clear-cut and high-bred in feature, with long black hair, and magnificent hazel eyes which looked round her presently in a charming amazement. Seashells and mother-of-pearl were worked into her cream-coloured tunic and tangled in her dark hair. A more perfect Naiad of the Deep could not be imagined, the very personification of the mystery and the glamour of the sea. We could see complete consciousness coming back into those marvellous eyes, and then she sprang suddenly to her feet with the activity of a young doe and ran to the side of the vessel. 'Cyrus! Cyrus!' she cried.

"We had already removed the anxiety of those below by a wireless. But now in quick succession each of them arrived, shooting thirty or forty feet into the air, and then falling back into the sea, from which we quickly raised them. All three were unconscious, and Scanlan was bleeding at the nose and ears, but within an hour all were able to totter to their feet. The first action of each was, I imagine, characteristic. Scanlan was led off by a laughing group to the bar, from which shouts of merriment are now resounding, much to the detriment of this composition. Dr. Maracot seized the bundle of papers, tore out one which consisted entirely, so far as I could judge, of algebraic symbols, and disappeared downstairs, while Cyrus Headley ran to the side of his strange maiden, and looks, by last reports, as if he had no intention of ever quitting it. Thus the matter stands, and we trust our weak wireless will carry our message as far as the Cape de Verde station. The fuller details of this wonderful adventure will come later, as is fitting, from the adventurers themselves."

CHAPTER VI

THERE are very many people who have written both to me, Cyrus Headley, Rhodes scholar of Oxford, and to Professor Maracot, and even to Bill Scanlan, since our very remarkable experience at the bottom of the Atlantic, where we were able at a point 200 miles southwest of the Canaries to make a submarine descent which has not only led to a revision of our views concerning deep-sea life and pressures, but has also established the survival of an old civilization under incredibly difficult conditions. In these letters we have been continually asked to give further details about our experiences. It will be understood that my original document was a very superficial one, and yet it covered most of the facts. There were some, however, which were withheld, and above all the tremendous episode of the Lord of the Dark Face. This involved some facts and some conclusions of so utterly extraordinary a nature that we all thought it was best to suppress it entirely for the present. Now, however, that Science has accepted our conclusions—and I may add since Society has accepted my bride—our general veracity is established and we may perhaps venture upon a narrative which might have repulsed public sympathy in the first instance. Before I get to the one tremendous happening I would lead up to it by some reminiscences of those wonderful months in the buried home of the Atlanteans, who by means of their vitrine oxygen bells are able to walk the ocean floor with the same ease as those Londoners whom I see now from my windows in the Hyde Park Hotel are strolling among the flower beds.

When first we were taken in by these people after our dreadful fall from the surface we were in the position of prisoners rather than of guests. I wish now to set upon record how this came to change and how through the splendour of Dr. Maracot we have left such a name down there that the memory of us will go down in their annals as of some celestial visitation. They knew nothing of our leaving, which they would certainly have prevented if they could, so that no doubt there is already a legend that we have returned to some heavenly sphere, taking with us the sweetest and choicest flower of their flock.

I would wish now to set down in their order some of the strange things of this wonderful world, and also some of the adventures which befell us until I came to the supreme adventure of all—one which will leave a mark upon each of us forever—the coming of the Lord of the Dark Face. In some ways I wish that we could have stayed longer in the Maracot Deep for there were many mysteries there, and up to the end there were things which we could not understand. Also we were rapidly learning something of their language, so that soon we should have had much more information.

Experience had taught these people what was terrible and what was innocent. One day, I remember, that there was a sudden alarm and that we all ran out in our oxygen bells on to the ocean bed, though why we ran or what we meant to do was a mystery to us. There could be no mistake, however, as to the horror and distraction upon the faces of those around us. When we got out on to the plain we met a number of the Greek coal-workers who were hastening towards the door of our Colony. They had come at such a pace and were so weary that they kept falling down in the ooze, and it was clear that we were really a rescue party for the purpose of picking up these cripples, and hurrying up the laggards. We saw no sign of weapons and no show of resistance against the coming danger. Soon the colliers were hustled along, and when the last one had been shoved through the door we looked back along the line that they had traversed. All that we could see was a couple of greenish wisplike clouds, luminous in the centre and ragged at the edges, which were drifting rather than moving in our direction. At the clear sight of them, though they were quite half a mile away, my companions were filled with panic and beat at the door so as to get in the sooner. It was surely nervous work to see these mysterious centres of trouble draw nearer, but the pumps acted swiftly and we were soon in safety once more. There was a great block of transparent crystal, ten feet long and two feet broad, above the lintel of the door, with lights so arranged that they threw a strong glare outside. Mounted on the ladders kept for the purpose, several of us, including myself, looked through this rude window. I saw the strange shimmering green circles of light pause before the door. As they did so the Atlanteans on either side of me simply gibbered with fear. Then one of the shadowy creatures outside came flickering up through the water and made for our crystal window. Instantly my companions pulled me down below the level of vision, but it seems that in my carelessness some of my hair did not get clear from whatever the maleficent influence may be which these strange creatures send forth. There is a patch there which is withered and white to this day.

It was not for a long time that the Atlanteans dared to open their door, and when at last a scout was sent forth he went amid hand-shakings and slaps on the back as one who does a gallant deed. His report was that all was clear, and soon joy had returned to the community and this strange visitation seemed to have been forgotten. We only gathered from the word "Praxa," repeated in various tones of horror, that this was the name of the creature. The only person who derived real joy from the incident was Professor Maracot, who could hardly be restrained from sallying out with a small net and a glass vase. "A new order of life, partly organic, partly gaseous, but clearly intelligent," was his general comment. "A freak out of Hell," was Scanlan's less scientific description.

Two days afterwards, when we were out on what we called a shrimping expedition, when we walked among the deep-sea foliage and captured in our handnets specimens of the smaller fish, we came suddenly upon the body of one of the coal-workers, who had no doubt been overtaken in his flight by these strange creatures. The glass bell had been broken—a matter which called for enormous strength, for this vitrine substance is extraordinarily tough, as you realized when you attempted to reach my first documents. The man's eyes had been torn out, but otherwise he had been uninjured.

"A dainty feeder!" said the Professor after our return. "There is a hawk parrot in New Zealand which will kill the lamb in order to get at a particular morsel of fat above the kidney. So this creature will slay the man for his eyes. In the heavens above and in the waters below, Nature knows but one law, and it is alas! remorseless cruelty."

We had many examples of that terrible law down there in the depths of the ocean. I can remember, for example, that many times we observed a curious groove upon the soft bathybian mud, as if a barrel had been rolled along it. We pointed it out to our Atlantean companions, and when we could interrogate them we tried to get from them some account of what this creature could be. As to its name our friends gave some of those peculiar clicking sounds which come into the Atlantean speech, and which cannot be reproduced either by the European tongue or by the European alphabet. Krixchok is perhaps an approximation to it. But as to its appearance we could always in such cases make use of the Atlantean thought reflector by which our friends were able to give a very clear vision of whatever was in their own minds. By this means they conveyed to us a picture of a very strange marine creature which the Professor could only classify as a gigantic sea slug. It seemed to be of great size, sausage-shaped, with eyes at the end of stems, and a thick coating of coarse hair or bristles. When showing this apparition, our friends by their gestures expressed the greatest horror and repulsion.

But this, as anyone could predicate who knew Maracot, only served to inflame his scientific passions and to make him the more eager to determine the exact species and sub-species of this unknown monster. Accordingly I was not surprised when, on the occasion of our next excursion, he stopped at the point where we clearly saw the mark of the brute upon the slime, and turned deliberately towards the tangle of sea-weed and basaltic blocks out of which it seemed to have come. The moment we left the plain the traces of course ceased, and yet there seemed to be a natural gully amid the rocks which clearly led to the den of the monster. We were all three armed with the pikes which the Atlanteans usually carried, but they seemed to me to be frail things with which to face unknown dangers. The Professor trudged ahead, however, and we could but follow after.

The rocky gorge ran upward, its sides formed of huge clusters of volcanic debris and draped with a profusion of the long red and black forms of lamellaria which are characteristic of the extreme depths of Ocean. A thousand beautiful ascidians and echinoderms of every joyous colour and fantastic shape peeped out from amid this herbage, which was alive with strange crustaceans and low forms of creeping life. Our progress was slow, for walking is never easy in the depths, and the angle up which we toiled was an acute one. Suddenly, however, we saw the creature whom we hunted, and the sight was not a reassuring one.

It was half protruded from its lair, which was a hollow in a basaltic pile. About five feet of hairy body was visible, and we perceived its eyes, which were as large as saucers, yellow in colour, and glittering like agates, moving round slowly upon their long pedicles as it heard the sound of our approach. Then slowly it began to unwind itself from its burrow, waving its heavy body along in caterpillar fashion. Once it reared up its head some four feet from the rocks, so as to have a better look at us, and I observed, as it did so, that it had what looked like the corrugated soles of tennis shoes fastened on either side of its neck, the same colour, size, and striped appearance. What this might mean I could not conjecture, but we were soon to have an object lesson in their use.

The Professor had braced himself with his pike projecting forward and a most determined expression upon his face. It was clear that the hope of a rare specimen had swept all fear from his mind. Scanlan and I were by no means so sure of ourselves, but we could not abandon the old man, so we stood our ground on either side of him. The creature, after that one long stare, began slowly and clumsily to make its way down the slope, worming its path among the rocks, and raising its pedicled eyes from time to time to see what we were about. It came so slowly that we seemed safe enough, since we could always out-distance it. And yet, had we only known it, we were standing very near to death.

It was surely Providence that sent us our warning. The beast was still making its lumbering approach, and may have been sixty yards from us, when a very large fish, a deep-sea groper, shot out from the algae jungle on our side of the gorge and swam slowly across it. It had reached the centre and was about midway between the creature and ourselves when it gave a convulsive leap, turned belly upward, and sank dead to the bottom of the ravine. At the same moment each of us felt an extraordinary and most unpleasant tingling pass over our whole bodies, while our knees seemed to give way beneath us. Old Maracot was as wary as he was audacious, and in an instant he had sized up the situation and realized that the game was up. We were faced by some creature which threw out electric waves to kill its prey, and our pikes were of no more use against it than against a machine-gun. Had it not been for the lucky chance that the fish drew its fire, we should have waited until it was near enough to loose off its full battery, which would infallibly have destroyed us. We blundered off as swiftly as we could, with the resolution to leave the giant electric sea-worm severely alone for the future.

These were some of the more terrible of the dangers of the deep. Yet another was the little black Hydrops ferox, as the Professor named him. He was a red fish not much longer than a herring, with a large mouth and a formidable row of teeth. He was harmless in ordinary circumstances, but the shedding of blood, even the very smallest amount of it, attracted him in an instant, and there was no possible salvation for the victim, who was torn to pieces by swarms of attackers. We saw a horrible sight once at the colliery pits, where a slave worker had the misfortune to cut his hand. In an instant, coming from all quarters, thousands of these fish were on to him. In vain he threw himself down and struggled; in vain his horrified companions beat them away with their picks and shovels. The lower part of him, beneath his bell, dissolved before our eyes amid the cloud of vibrant life which surrounded him. One instant we saw a man. The next there was a red mass with white protruding bones. A minute later the bones only were left below the waist and half a clean-picked skeleton was lying at the bottom of the sea. The sight was so horrifying that we were all ill, and the hard-boiled Scanlan actually fell down in a faint and we had some difficulty in getting him home.

But the strange sights which we saw were not always horrifying. I have in mind one which will never fade from our memory. It was on one of those excursions which we delighted to take, sometimes with an Atlantean guide, and sometimes by ourselves when our hosts had learned that we did not need constant attendance and nursing. We were passing over a portion of the plain with which we were quite familiar, when we perceived, to our surprise, that a great patch of light yellow sand, half an acre or so in extent, had been laid down or uncovered since our last visit. We were standing in some surprise, wondering what submarine current or seismic movement could have brought this about, when to our absolute amazement the whole thing rose up and swam with slow undulations immediately above our heads. It was so huge that the great canopy took some appreciable time, a minute or two, to pass from over us. It was a gigantic flat fish, not different, so far as the Professor could observe, from one of our own little dabs, but grown to this enormous size upon the nutritious food which the bathybian deposits provide. It vanished away into the darkness above us, a great glimmering, flickering white and yellow expanse, and we saw it no more.

There was one other phenomenon of the deep sea which was very unexpected. That was the tornadoes which frequently occur. They seem to be caused by the periodical arrival of violent submarine currents which set in with little warning and are terrific while they last, causing as much confusion and destruction as the highest wind would do upon land. No doubt without these visitations there would be that putridity and stagnation which absolute immobility must give, so that, as in all Nature's processes, there was an excellent object in view; but the experience none the less was an alarming one.

On the first occasion when I was caught in such a watery cyclone, I had gone out with that very dear lady to whom I have alluded, Mona, the daughter of Manda. There was a very beautiful bank loaded with algae of a thousand varied colours which lay a mile or so from the Colony. This was Mona's very special garden which she greatly loved, a tangle of pink serpularia, purple ophiurids, and red holothurians. On this day she had taken me to see it, and it was while we were standing before it that the storm burst. So strong was the current which suddenly flowed upon us that it was only by holding together and getting behind the shelter of rocks that we could save ourselves from being washed away. I observed that this rushing stream of water was quite warm, almost as warm as one could bear, which may show that there is a volcanic origin in these disturbances and that they are the wash from some submarine disturbance in some far-off region of the ocean bed. The mud of the great plain was stirred up by the rush of the current, and the light was darkened by the thick cloud of matter suspended in the water around us. To find our way back was impossible, for we had lost all sense of direction, and in any case could hardly move against the rush of the water. Then on the top of all else a slowly increasing heaviness of the chest and difficulty of breathing warned me that our oxygen supply was beginning to fail us.

It is at such times, when we are in the immediate presence of death, that the great primitive passions float to the surface and submerge all our lesser emotions. It was only at that moment that I knew that I loved my gentle companion, loved her with all my heart and soul, loved her with a love which was rooted deep down and was part of my very self. How strange a thing is a love like that! How impossible to analyze! It was not for her face or figure, lovely as they were. It was not for her voice, though it was more musical than any I have known, nor was it for mental communion, since I could only learn her thoughts from her sensitive, ever-changing face. No, it was something at the back of her dark dreamy eyes, something in the very depths of her soul as of mine which made us mates for all time. I held out my hand and clasped her own, reading in her face that there was no thought or emotion of mine which was not flooding her own receptive mind and flushing her lovely cheek. Death at my side would present no terror to her, and as for myself my heart throbbed at the very thought.

But it was not to be. One would think that our glass coverings excluded sounds, but as a matter of fact the throb of certain air vibrations penetrated them easily, or by their impact started similar vibrations within. There was a loud beat, a reverberating clang, like that of a distant gong. I had no idea what it might mean, but my companion was in no doubt. Still holding my hand, she rose from our shelter, and after listening intently she crouched down and began to make her way against the storm. It was a race against death, for every instant the terrible oppression on my chest became more unbearable. I saw her dear face peering most anxiously into mine, and I staggered on in the direction to which she led me. Her appearance and her movements showed that her oxygen supply was less exhausted than mine. I held on as long as Nature would allow, and then suddenly everything swam around me. I threw out my arms and fell senseless upon the soft ocean floor.

When I came to myself I was lying on my own couch inside the Atlantean Palace. The old yellow-clad priest was standing beside me, a phial of some stimulant in his hand. Maracot and Scanlan, with distressed faces, were bending over me, while Mona knelt at the bottom of the bed with tender anxiety upon her features. It seems that the brave girl had hastened on to the community door, from which on occasions of this sort it was the custom to beat a great gong as a guide to any wanderers who might be lost. There she had explained my position and had guided back the rescue party, including my two comrades, who had brought me back in their arms. Whatever I may do in life, it is truly Mona who will do it; for that life has been a gift from her.

Now that by a miracle she has come to join me in the upper world, the human world under the sky, it is strange to reflect upon the fact that my love was such that I was willing, most willing, to remain forever in the depths so long as she should be all my own. For long I could not understand that deep, deep intimate bond which held us together, and which was felt, as I could see, as strongly by her as by me. It was Manda, her father, who gave me an explanation which was as unexpected as it was satisfying.

He had smiled gently over our love affair—smiled with the indulgent, half-amused air of one who sees that come to pass which he had already anticipated. Then one day he led me aside and in his own chamber he placed that silver screen upon which his thoughts and knowledge could be reflected. Never while the breath of life is in my body can I forget that which he showed me—and her. Seated side by side, our hands clasped together, we watched entranced while the pictures flickered up before our eyes, formed and projected by that racial memory of the past which these Atlanteans possess.

There was a rocky peninsula jutting out into a lovely blue ocean. I may not have told you before that in these thought cinemas, if I may use the expression, colour is produced as well as form. On this headland was a house of quaint design, wide-spread, red-roofed, white-walled, and beautiful. A grove of palm trees surrounded it. In this grove there appeared to be a camp, for we could see the white sheen of tents and here and there the glimmer of arms as of some sentinel keeping ward. Out of this grove there walked a middle-aged man clad in mail armour, with a round light shield on his arm. He carried something in his other hand, but whether sword or javelin I could not see. He turned his face towards us once, and I saw at once that he was of the same breed as the Atlantean men who were around me. Indeed, he might have been the twin brother of Manda, save that his features were harsh and menacing—a brute man, but one who was brutal not from ignorance but from the trend of his own nature. The brute and the brain are surely the most dangerous of all combinations. In this high forehead and sardonic, bearded mouth one sensed the very essence of evil. If this were indeed some previous incarnation of Manda himself, and by his gestures he seemed to wish us to understand that it was, then in soul, if not in mind, he has risen far since then.

As he approached the house, we saw in the picture that a young woman came out to meet him. She was clad as the old Greeks were clad, in a long clinging white garment, the simplest and yet the most beautiful and dignified dress that woman has ever yet devised. Her manner as she approached the man was one of submission and reverence—the manner of a dutiful daughter to a father. He repulsed her savagely, however; raising his hand as if to strike her. As she shrank back from him, the sun lit up her beautiful tearful face and I saw it was my Mona.

The silver screen blurred, and an instant later another scene was forming. It was a rock-bound cove, which I sensed to belong to that very peninsula which I had already seen. A strange-shaped boat with high pointed ends was in the foregound. It was night, but the moon shone very brightly on the water. The familiar stars, the same to Atlantis as to us, glittered in the sky. Slowly and cautiously the boat drew in. There were two rowers, and in the bows was a man enveloped in a dark cloak. As he came close to the shore he stood up and looked eagerly around him. I saw his pale, earnest face in the clear moonlight. It did not need the convulsive clasp of Mona or the ejaculation of Manda to explain that strange intimate thrill which shot over me as I looked. The man was myself.

Yes, I, Cyrus Headley, now of New York and of Oxford; I, the latest product of modern culture, had myself once been part of this mighty civilization of old. I understood now why many of the symbols and hieroglyphs which I had seen around me had impressed me with a vague familiarity. Again and again I had felt like a man who strains his memory because he feels that he is on the edge of some great discovery, which is always awaiting him, and yet is always just outside his grasp. Now, too, I understood that deep soul thrill which I had encountered when my eyes met those of Mona. They came from the depths of my own subconscious self where the memories of twelve thousand years still lingered.

Now the boat had touched the shore, and out of the bushes above there had come a glimmering white figure. My arms were outstretched to enfold it. After one hurried embrace I had half-lifted, half-carried her into the boat. But now there was a sudden alarm. With frantic gestures I beckoned to the rowers to push out. It was too late. Men swarmed out of the bushes. Eager hands seized the side of the boat. In vain I tried to beat them off. An axe gleamed in the air and crashed down upon my head. I fell forward dead upon the lady, bathing her white robe in my blood. I saw her screaming, wild-eyed and open-mouthed, while her father dragged her by her long black hair from underneath my body. Then the curtain closed down.

Once again a picture flickered up upon the silver screen. It was the inside of the house of refuge which had been built by the wise Atlantean for a place of refuge on the day of doom—that very house in which we now stood. I saw its crowded, terrified inmates at the moment of the catastrophe. There I saw my Mona once again, and there also was her father who had learned better and wiser ways so that he was now included among those who might be saved. We saw the great hall rocking like a ship in a storm, while the awestruck refugees clung to the pillars or fell upon the floor. Then we saw the lurch and fall as it descended through the waves. Once more the scene died away, and Manda turned, smiling, to show that all was over.

Yes, we had lived before, the whole group of us, Manda and Mona and I, and perhaps shall live again, acting and reacting down the long chain of our lives. I had died in the upper world, and so my own reincarnations had been upon that plane. Manda and Mona had died under the waves, and so it was there that their cosmic destiny had been worked out. We had for a moment seen a corner lifted in the great dark veil of Nature and had one passing gleam of truth amid the mysteries which surround us. Each life is but one chapter in a story which God has designed. You cannot judge its wisdom or its justice until in some supreme day from some pinnacle of knowledge you look back and see at last the cause and the effect, acting and reacting, down all the long chronicles of Time.

This new-found and delightful relationship of mine may have saved us all a little later when the only serious quarrel which we ever had broke out between us and the community with which we dwelt. As it was, it might have gone ill with us had not a far greater matter come to engage the attention of all, and to place on us a pinnacle in their estimation. It came about thus.

One morning, if such a term can be used where the time of day could only be judged by our occupations, the Professor and I were seated in our large common room. He had fitted one corner of it as a laboratory and was busily engaged in dissecting a gastrostomus which he had netted the day before. On his table were scattered a litter of amphipods and copepods with specimens of Valella, Ianthina, Physalia, and a hundred other creatures whose smell was by no means as attractive as their appearance. I was seated near him studying an Atlantean grammar, for our friends had plenty of books printed in curious right-to-left fashion upon what I thought was parchment but which proved to be the bladders of fishes, pressed and preserved. I was bent on getting the key which would unlock all this knowledge, and therefore I spent much of my time over the alphabet and the elements of the language.

Suddenly, however our peaceful pursuits were rudely interrupted by an extraordinary procession which rushed into the room. First came Bill Scanlan, very red and excited, one arm waving in the air, and, to our amazement, a plump and noisy baby under the other. Behind him was Berbrix, the Atlantean engineer who had helped Scanlan to erect the wireless receiver. He was a large stout jovial man as a rule, but now his big fat face was convulsed with grief. Behind him again was a woman whose straw-coloured hair and blue eyes showed that she was no Atlantean but one of the subordinate race which we traced to the ancient Greeks.

"Look it here, boss," cried the excited Scanlan. "This guy Berbrix, who is a regular fellar, is going clean goofie and so is this skirt whom he has married, and I guess it is up to us to see that they get a square deal. Far as I understand it she is like a nigger would be down South, and he said a mouthful when he asked her to marry him, but I reckon that's the guy's own affair and nothing to us."

"Of course it is his own affair," said I. "What on earth has bitten you, Scanlan?"

"It's like this, boss. Here has a baby come along. It seems the folk here don't want a breed of that sort nohow, and the priests are out to offer up the baby to that dumb image down yonder. The chief high muck-a-muck got hold of the baby and was sailin' off with it but Berbrix yanked it away, and I threw him down on his ear-hole, and now the whole pack are at our heels and——"

Scanlan got no further with his explanation, for there was a shouting and a rush of feet in the passage, our door was flung open, and several of the yellow-clad attendants of the Temple rushed into the room. Behind them, fierce and austere, came the high-nosed formidable priest. He beckoned with his hand, and his servants rushed forward to seize the child. They halted, however, in indecision as they saw Scanlan throw the baby down among the specimens on the table behind him, and pick up a pike with which he confronted his assailants. They had drawn their knives so I also ran with a pike to Scanlan's aid, while Berbrix did the same. So menacing were we that the Temple servants shrank back and things seemed to have come to a deadlock.

"Mr. Headley, sir, you speak a bit of their lingo," cried Scanlan. "Tell them there ain't no soft picking here. Tell them we ain't givin' away no babies this morning, thank you. Tell them there will be such a rough house as they never saw if they don't vamose the ranche. There, now, you asked for it and you've got it good and plenty and I wish you joy."

The latter part of Scanlan's speech was caused by the fact that Dr. Maracot had suddenly plunged the scalpel with which he was performing his dissection into the arm of one of the attendants who had crept round and had raised his knife to stab Scanlan. The man howled and danced about in fear and pain while his comrades, incited by the old priest, prepared to make a rush. Heaven only knows what would have happened if Manda and Mona had not entered the room. He stared with amazement at the scene and asked a number of eager questions from the High Priest. Mona had come over to me, and with a happy inspiration I picked up the baby and placed it in her arms where it settled down and cooed most contentedly.

Manda's brow was overcast and it was clear that he was greatly puzzled what to do. He sent the Priest and his satellites back to the Temple, and then he entered into a long explanation only a part of which I could understand and pass on to my companions.

"You are to give up the baby," I said to Scanlan.

"Give it up! No, sir. Nothin' doing!"

"This lady is to take charge of mother and child."

"That's another matter. If Miss Mona takes it on I am contented. But if that bindlestiff of a priest——"

"No, no, he cannot interfere. The matter is to be referred to the Council. It is very serious, for I understand Manda to say that the Priest is within his rights and that it is an old-established custom of the nation. They could never, he says, distinguish between the upper and lower races if they had all sorts of intermediates in between. If children are born they must die. That is the law."

"Well, this baby won't die anyhow."

"I hope not. He said he would do all he could with the Council. But it will be a week or two before they meet. So it's safe up to then, and who knows what may happen in the meantime?"

Yes, who knew what might happen? Who could have dreamed what *did* happen? Out of this is fashioned the next chapter of our adventures.

CHAPTER VII

I HAVE already said that within a short distance of the underground dwelling of the Atlanteans, prepared beforehand to meet the catastrophe which overwhelmed their native land, there lay the ruins of that great city of which their dwelling had once been part. I have described also how with the vitrine bells charged with oxygen upon our heads we were taken to visit this place, and I tried to convey how deep were our emotions as we viewed it. No words can describe the tremendous impression produced by those colossal ruins, the huge carved pillars and gigantic buildings, all lying stark and silent in the gray phosphorescent light of the bathybian deeps, with no movement save the slow wash of the giant fronds in the deep-sea currents, or the flickering shadows of the great fish which passed through the gaping doors or flitted round the dismantled chambers. It was a favourite haunt of ours, and under the guidance of our friend Manda we passed many an hour examining the strange architecture and all the other remains of that vanished civilization which bore every sign of having been, so far as material knowledge goes, far ahead of our own.

I have said material knowledge. Soon we were to have proof that in spiritual culture there was a vast chasm which separated them from us. The lesson which we carry from their rise and their fall is that the greatest danger which can come to a state is when its intellect outruns its soul. It destroyed this old civilization, and it may yet be the ruin of our own. We had observed that in one part of the ancient city there was a large building which must have stood upon a hill, for it was still considerably elevated above the general level. A long flight of broad steps constructed from black marble led up to it, and the same material had been used in most of the building, but it was nearly obscured now by a horrible yellow fungus, a fleshy leprous mass, which hung down from every cornice and projection. Above the main doorway, carved also in black marble, was a terrible Medusa-like head with radiating serpents, and the same symbol was repeated here and there upon the walls. Several times we had wished to explore this sinister building, but on each occasion our friend Manda had shown the greatest agitation and by frantic gestures had implored us to turn away. It was clear that so long as he was in our company we should never have our way, and yet a great curiosity urged us to penetrate the secret of this ominous place. We held a council on the matter one morning, Bill Scanlan and I.

"Look it here, Bo," said he, "there is something there that this guy does not want us to see, and the more he hides it the more of a hunch have I that I want to be set wise to it. We don't need no guides any more, you or I. I guess we can put on our own glass tops and walk out of the front door same as any other citizen. Let us go down and explore."

"Why not?" said I, for I was as curious about the matter as Scanlan. "Do you see any objection, sir?" I asked, for Dr. Maracot had entered the room. "Perhaps you would care to come down with us and fathom the mystery of the Palace of Black Marble."

"It may be the Palace of Black Magic as well," said he. "Did you ever hear of the Lord of the Dark Face?"

I confessed that I never did. I forget if I have said before that the Professor was a world-famed specialist on Comparative Religions and ancient primitive beliefs. Even the distant Atlantis was not beyond the range of his learning.

"Our knowledge of the conditions there came to us chiefly by the way of Egypt," said he. "It is what the Priests of the Temple at Sais told Solon which is the solid nucleus round which all the rest, part fact and part fiction, has gathered."

"And what wise cracks did the priests say?" asked Scanlan.

"Well, they said a good deal. But among other things they handed down a legend of the Lord of the Dark Face. I can't help thinking that he may have been the Master of the Black Marble Palace. Some say that there were several Lords of the Dark Face— but one at least is on record."

"And what sort of a duck was he?" asked Scanlan.

"Well, by all accounts, he was more than a man, both in his power and in his wickedness. Indeed, it was on account of these things, and on account of the utter corruption which he had brought upon the people, that the whole land was destroyed."

"Like Sodom and Gomorrah."

"Exactly. There would seem to be a point where things become impossible. Nature's patience is exhausted, and the only course open is to smear it all out and begin again. This creature, one can hardly call him a man, had trafficked in unholy arts and had acquired magic powers of the most far-reaching sort which he turned to evil ends. That is the legend of the Lord of the Dark Face. It would explain why his house is still a thing of horror to these poor people and why they dread that we should go near it."

"Which makes me the more eager to do so," I cried.

"Same here, Bo," Bill added.

"I confess that I too, should be interested to examine it," said the Professor. "I cannot see that our kind hosts here will be any the worse if we make a little expedition of our own, since their superstition makes it difficult for them to accompany us. We will take our opportunity and do so."

It was some little time before that opportunity came, for our small community was so closely knit that there was little privacy in life. It chanced, however, one morning—so far as we could with our rough calendar reckon night and morning—there was some religious observance which assembled them all and took up all their attention. The chance was too good for us to miss, and having assured the two janitors who worked the great pumps of the entrance chamber that all was right we soon found ourselves alone upon the ocean bed and bound for the old city. Progress is slow through the heavy medium of salt water, and even a short walk is wearying, but within an hour we found ourselves in front of the huge black building which had excited our curiosity. With no friendly guide to check us, and no presentiment of danger, we ascended the marble stair and passed through the huge carved portals of this palace of evil.

It was far better preserved than the other buildings of the old city—so much so, indeed, that the stone shell was in no way altered, and only the furniture and the hangings had long decayed and vanished. Nature, however, had brought her own hangings, and very horrible they were. It was a gloomy, shadowy place at the best, but in those hideous shadows lurked the obscene shapes of monstrous polyps and strange, misformed fish which were like the creations of a nightmare. Especially I remember an enormous purple seaslug which crawled, in great numbers, everywhere and large black flat fish which lay like mats upon the floor, with long waving tentacles tipped with flame vibrating above them in the water. We had to step carefully, for the whole building was filled with hideous creatures which might well prove to be as poisonous as they looked.

There were richly ornamented passages with small side rooms leading out from them, but the centre of the building was taken up by one magnificent hall, which in the days of its grandeur must have been one of the most wonderful chambers ever erected by human hands. In that gloomy light we could see neither the roof nor the full sweep of the walls, but as we walked round, our lamps casting tunnels of light before us, we appreciated its huge proportions and the marvellous decorations of the walls. These decorations took the form of statues and ornaments, carved with the highest perfection of art, but horrible and revolting in their subjects. All that the most depraved human mind could conceive of Sadic cruelty and bestial lust was reproduced upon the walls. Through the shadows monstrous images and horrible imaginings loomed round us on every side. If ever the devil had a temple erected in his honour, it was there. So, too, was the devil himself, for at one end of the room, under a canopy of discoloured metal which may well have been gold, and on a high throne of red marble, there was seated a dreadful deity, the very impersonation of evil, savage, scowling, and relentless, modelled upon the same lines as the Baal whom we had seen in the Atlantean Colony, but infinitely stranger and more repulsive. There was a fascination in the wonderful vigour of that terrible countenance, and we were standing with our lamps playing upon it, absorbed in our reflections, when the most amazing, the most incredible thing came to break in upon our reflections. From behind us there came the sound of a loud, derisive human laugh.

Our heads were, as I have explained, enclosed in our glass bells, from which all sound was excluded, nor was it possible for anyone wearing a bell to utter any sound. And yet that mocking laugh fell clear upon the ears of each of us. We sprang round and stood amazed at what was before us.

Against one of the pillars of the hall a man was leaning, his arms folded upon his chest and his malevolent eyes fixed with a threatening glare upon ourselves. I have called him a man, but he was unlike any man whom I have ever seen, and the fact that he both breathed and talked as no man could breathe or talk, and made his voice carry as no human voice could carry, told us that he had that in him which made him very different from ourselves. Outwardly he was a magnificent creature, not less than seven feet in height and built upon the lines of a perfect athlete, which was the more noticeable as he wore a costume which fitted tightly upon his figure, and seemed to consist of glazed black leather. His face was that of a bronze statue—a statue wrought by some master craftsman in order to depict all the power and also all the evil which the human features could portray. It was not bloated or sensual, for such characteristics would have meant weakness and there was no trace of weakness there. On the contrary, it was extraordinarily clean-cut and aquiline, with an eagle nose, dark bristling brows, and smouldering black eyes which flashed and glowed with an inner fire. It was those remorseless, malignant eyes, and the beautiful but cruel, straight, hard-lipped mouth, set like fate, which gave the terror to his face. One felt, as one looked at him, that magnificent as he was in his person, he was evil to the very marrow, his glance a threat, his smile a sneer, his laugh a mockery.

"Well, gentlemen," he said, talking excellent English in a voice which sounded as clear as if we were all back upon earth. "You have had a remarkable adventure in the past and are likely to have an even more exciting one in the future, though it may be my pleasant task to bring it to a sudden end. This, I fear, is a rather one-sided conversation, but as I am perfectly well able to read your thoughts, and as I know all about you, you need not fear any misunderstanding. But you have a great deal—a very great deal to learn."

We looked at each other in helpless amazement. It was hard, indeed, to be prevented from comparing notes as to our reactions to this amazing development. Again we heard that rasping laugh.

"Yes, it is indeed hard. But you can talk when you return, for I wish you to return and to take a message with you. If it were not for that message, I think that this visit to my home would have been your end. But first of all I have a few things which I wished to say to you. I will address you, Dr. Maracot, as the oldest and presumably the wisest of the party, though none could have been very wise to make such an excursion as this. You hear me very well, do you not? That is right, a nod or a shake is all I ask.

"Of course you know who I am. I fancy you discovered me lately. No one can speak or think of me that I do not know it. No one can come into this my old home, my innermost intimate shrine, that I am not summoned. That is why these poor wretches down yonder avoid it, and wanted you to avoid it also. You would have been wiser if you had followed their advice. You have brought me to you, and when once I am brought I do not readily leave.

"Your mind with its little grain of earth science is

worrying itself over the problems which I present. How is it that I can live here without oxygen? I do not live here. I live in the great world of men under the light of the sun. I only come here when I am called as you have called me. But I am an ether-breathing creature. There is as much ether here as on a mountain top. Some of your own people can live without air. The cataleptic lies for months and never breathes. I am even as he, but I remain, as you see me, conscious and active.

"Now you worry as to how you can hear me. Is it not the very essence of wireless transmission that it turns from the ether to the air? So I, too, can turn my words from my etheric utterance to impinge upon your ears through the air which fills those clumsy bells of yours.

"And my English? Well, I hope it is fairly good. I have lived some time on earth, oh, a weary, weary time. How long is it? Is this the eleven thousandth or the twelve thousandth year? The latter, I think. I have had time to learn all human tongues. My English is no better than the rest.

"Have I resolved some of your doubts? That is right. I can see if I cannot hear you. But now I have something more serious to say."

"I am Baal-seepa. I am the Lord of the Dark Face. I am he who went so far into the inner secrets of Nature that I could defy Death himself. I have so handled things that I could not die if I would. Some will stronger than my own is to be found if I am ever to die. Oh, mortals, never pray to be delivered from death. It may seem terrible, but eternal life is infinitely more so. To go on and on and on while the endless procession of humanity goes past you. To sit ever at the wayside of history and to see it go, ever moving onward and leaving you behind. Is it a wonder that my heart is black and bitter, and that I curse the whole foolish drove of them? I injure them when I can. Why should I not?

"You wonder how I can injure them. I have powers, and they are not small ones. I can sway the minds of men. I am the master of the mob. Where evil has been planned there have I ever been. I was with the Huns when they laid half Europe in ruins. I was with the Saracens when under the name of religion they put to the sword all who gainsayed them. I was out on Bartholomew's night. I lay behind the slave trade. It was my whisper which burned ten thousand old crones whom the fools called witches. I was the tall dark man who led the mob in Paris when the streets swam in blood. Rare times those, but they have been even better of late in Russia. That is whence I have come. I had half-forgotten this colony of sea rats who burrow under the mud and carry on a few of the arts and legends of that grand land where life flourished as never since. It is you who reminded me of them, for this old home of mine is still united, by personal vibrations of which your science knows nothing, to the man who built and loved it. I knew that strangers had entered it, I inquired, and here I am. So now since I *am* here—and it is the first time for a thousand years—it has reminded me of these people. They have lingered long enough. It is time for them to go. They are sprung from the power of one who defied me in his life, and who built up this means of escape from the catastrophe which engulfed all but his people and myself. His wisdom saved them and my powers saved me. But now my powers will crush those whom he saved, and the story will be complete."

He put his hand into his breast and he took out a piece of script. "You will give this to the chief of the waterrats," said he. "I regret that you gentlemen should share their fate, but since you are the primary cause of their misfortune it is only justice, after all. I will see you again later. Meanwhile, I would commend a study of these pictures and carvings, which will give you some idea of the height to which I had raised Atlantis during the days of my rule. Here you will find some record of the manners and customs of the people when under my influence. Life was very varied, very highly coloured, very many-sided. In these drab days they would call it an orgy of wickedness. Well, call it what you will, I brought it about, I rejoiced in it, and I have no regrets. Had I my time again, I would do even so and more, save only for this fatal gift of eternal life. Warda, whom I curse and whom I should have killed before he grew strong enough to turn people against me, was wiser than I in this. He still revisits earth, but it is as a spirit, not a man. And now I go. You came here from curiosity, my friends. I can but trust that that curiosity is satisfied."

And then we saw him disappear. Yes, before our very eyes he vanished. It was not done in an instant. He stood clear of the pillar against which he had been leaning. His splendid towering figure seemed blurred at the edges. The light died out of his eyes and his features grew indistinct. Then in a moment he had become a dark whirling cloud which swept upward through the stagnant water of this dreadful hall. Then he was gone, and we stood gazing at each other and marvelling at the strange possibilities of life.

We did not linger in that horrible palace. It was not a safe place in which to loiter. As it was I picked one of those noxious purple slugs off the shoulder of Bill Scanlan, and I was myself badly stung in the hand by the venom spat at me by a great yellow lamelli branch. As we staggered out I had one last impression of those dreadful carvings, the devil's own handiwork, upon the walls, and then we almost ran down the darksome passage, cursing the day that ever we had been fools enough to enter it. It was joy indeed to be out in the phosphorescent light of the bathybian plain, and to see the clear translucent water once again around us. Within an hour we were back in our home once more. With our helmets removed, we met in consultation in our own chamber. The Professor and I were too overwhelmed with it all to be able to put our thoughts into words. It was only the irrepressible vitality of Bill Scanlan which rose superior.

"Holy smoke!" said he. "We are up against it now. I guess this guy is the big noise out of hell. Seems to me, with his pictures and statues and the rest, he would make the wardsman of a red-light precinct look like two cents. How to handle him—that's the question."

Dr. Maracot was lost in thought. Then he rang the bell and summoned our yellow-clad attendant. "Manda," said he. A minute later our friend was in the room. Maracot handed him the fateful letter.

Never have I admired a man as I did Manda at that moment. We had brought threatened ruin upon his people and himself by our unjustifiable curiosity—we, the strangers whom he had rescued when everything was hopelessly lost. And yet, though he turned a ghastly colour as he read the message, there was no touch of reproach in the sad brown eyes which turned upon us. He shook his head, and despair was in every gesture. "Baal-seepa! Baal-seepa!" he cried, and pressed his hands convulsively to his eyes, as if shutting out some horrible vision. He ran about the room like a man distracted with his grief, and finally rushed away to read the fatal message to the community. We heard a few minutes later the clang of the great bell which summoned them all to conference in the Central Hall.

"Shall we go?" I asked.

Dr. Maracot shook his head.

"What can we do? For that matter, what can they do? What chance have they against one who has the powers of a demon?"

"As much chance as a bunch of rabbits against a weasel," said Scanlan. "But, by Gosh, it's up to us to find a way out. I guess we can't go out of our way to raise the devil and then pass the buck to the folk that saved us."

"What do you suggest?" I asked eagerly, for behind all his slang and his levity I recognized the strong, practical ability of this modern man of his hands.

"Well, you can search me," said he. "And yet maybe this guy is not as safe as he thinks. A bit of it may have got worn out with age, and he's getting on in years if we can take his word for it."

"You think we might attack him?"

"Lunacy!" interjected the Doctor.

Scanlan went to his locker. When he faced round he had a big six-shooter in his hand.

"What about this?" he said. "I laid hold of it when we got our chance at the wreck. I thought maybe it might come in useful. I've a dozen shells here. Maybe if I made as many holes in the big stiff it would let out some of his magic. Lord save us! What is it?"

The revolver clattered down upon the floor, and Scanlan was writhing in agonies of pain, his left hand clasping his right wrist. Terrible cramps had seized his arm, and as we tried to alleviate them we could feel the muscles knotted up as hard as the roots of a tree. The sweat of agony streamed down the poor fellow's brow. Finally, utterly cowed and exhausted, he fell upon his bed.

"That lets me out," he said. "I'm through. Yes, thank you, the pain is better. But it is K.O. to William Scanlan. I've learned my lesson. You don't fight hell with six-shooters, and it's no use to try. I give him best from now onward."

"Yes, you have had your lesson," said Maracot, "and it has been a severe one."

"Then you think our case is hopeless?"

"What can we do when, as it would seem, he is aware of every word and action? And yet we will not despair." He sat in thought for a few moments. "I think," he resumed, "that you, Scanlan, had best lie where you are for a time. You have had a shock from which it will take you some time to recover."

"If there is anything doing, count me in, though I guess we can cut out the rough stuff," said our comrade bravely, but his drawn face and shaking limbs showed what he had endured.

"There is nothing doing so far as you are concerned. We at least have learned what is the wrong way to go to work. All violence is useless. We are working on another plane—the plane of spirit. Do you remain here, Headley. I am going to the room which I use as a study. Perhaps if I were alone I could see a little more clearly what we should do."

Both Scanlan and I had learned to have a great confidence in Maracot. If any human brain could solve our difficulties, it would be his. And yet surely we had reached a point which was beyond all human capacity. We were as helpless as children in the face of forces which we could neither understand nor control. Scanlan had fallen into a troubled sleep. My own one thought as I sat beside him was not how we should escape, but rather what form the blow would take and when it would fall. At any moment I was prepared to see the solid roof above us sink in, the walls collapse, and the dark waters of the lowest deep close in upon those who had defied them so long.

Then suddenly the great bell pealed out once more. Its harsh clamour jarred upon every nerve. I sprang to my feet, and Scanlan sat up in bed. It was no ordinary summons which rang through the old palace. The agitated tumultuous ringing, broken and irregular, was calling an alarm. All had to come, and at once. It was menacing and insistent. "Come now! Come at once! Leave everything and come!" cried the bell.

"Say, Bo, we should be with them," said Scanlan. "I guess they're up against it now."

"And yet what can we do?"

"Maybe just the sight of us will give them a bit of heart. Anyhow, they must not think that we are quitters. Where is the Doc?"

"He went to his study. But you are right, Scanlan. We should be with the others and let them see that we are ready to share their fate."

"The poor boobs seem to lean on us in a way. It may be that they know more than we, but we seem to have more sand in our craw than they. I guess they have taken what was given to them, and we have had to find things for ourselves. Well, it's time for the deluge—if the deluge has got to be."

But as we approached the door a most unexpected interruption detained us. Dr. Maracot stood before us. But was it indeed the Dr. Maracot whom we had known--this self-assured man with strength and resolution shining from every feature of his masterful face? The quiet scholar had been submerged, and here was a superman, a great leader, a dominant soul who might mould mankind to his desires.

"Yes, friends, we shall be needed. All may yet be well. But come at once, or it may be too late. I will explain everything later—if there is any later for us. Yes, yes, we are coming."

The latter words, with appropriate gesture, were spoken to some terrified Atlanteans who had appeared at the door and were eagerly beckoning to us to come. It was a fact, as Scanlan had said, that we had shown ourselves several times to be stronger in character and prompter in action than these secluded people, and now at this hour of supreme danger they seemed to cling to us. I could hear a subdued murmur of satisfaction and relief as we entered the crowded hall and took the places reserved for us in the front row.

It was time that we came, if we were indeed to bring any help. The terrible presence was already standing upon the dais and facing with a cruel, thin-lipped, demoniacal smile the cowering folk before him. Scanlan's simile of a bunch of rabbits before a weasel came back to my memory as I looked round at them. They sank together, holding on to each other in their terror, and gazing wide-eyed at the mighty figure which cowered above them and the ruthless granite-hewed face which looked down upon them. Never can I forget the impression of those semicircular rows, tier above tier, of haggard, wild-eyed faces with their horrified gaze all directed towards the central dais. It would seem that he had already pronounced their doom and that they stood in the shadow of death waiting for its fulfilment. Manda was standing in abject submission, pleading in broken accents for his people, but one could see that his words only gave an added zest to the monster who stood sneering before him. The creature interrupted him with a few rasping words, and raised his right hand in the air, while a cry of despair rose from the assembly.

And at that moment Dr. Maracot sprang upon the dais. It was amazing to watch him. Some miracle seemed to have altered the man. He had the gait and the gesture of a youth, and yet upon his face there was a look of such power as I have never seen upon human features yet. He strode up to the swarthy giant, who glared down at him in amazement.

"Well, little man, what have you to say?" he asked.

"I have this to say," said Maracot. "Your time has come. You have over-stayed it. Go down! Go down into the Hell that has been waiting for you so long. You are a prince of darkness. Go where the darkness is."

The demon's eyes shot dark fire as he answered:

"When my time comes, if it should ever come, it will not be from the lips of a wretched mortal that I shall learn it," said he. "What power have you that you could oppose for a moment one who is in the secret places of Nature? I could blast you where you stand."

Maracot looked into those terrible eyes without blenching. It seemed to me that it was the giant who flinched away from his gaze.

"Unhappy being," said Maracot. "It is I who have the power and the will to blast you where you stand. Too long have you cursed the world with your presence. You have been a plague-spot infecting all that was beautiful and good. The hearts of men will be lighter when you are gone and the sun will shine more brightly."

"What is this? Who are you? What is it that you are saying?" stammered the creature.

"You speak of secret knowledge. Shall I tell you that which is at the very base of it? It is that on every plane the good of that plane can be stronger than the evil. The angel will still beat the devil. For the moment I am on the same plane on which you have so long been, and I hold the power of the conqueror. It has been given to me. So again I say, down with you! Down to Hell to which you belong! Down, sir! Down, I say! Down!"

And then the miracle occurred. For a minute or more—how can one count time at such moments?—two beings, the mortal and the demon, faced each other as rigid as statues, glaring into each other's eyes with inexorable will upon the two faces, the dark one and the fair. Then suddenly the great creature flinched. His face convulsed with rage, he threw two clawing hands up into the air. "It is you, Warda, you cursed one! I recognize your handiwork. Oh, curse you, Warda. Curse you! Curse you!" His voice died away, his long dark figure became blurred in its outline, his head dropped upon his chest, his knees sagged under him, down he sank and down, and as he sank he changed his shape. At first it was a crouching human being, then it was a dark formless mass, and then with sudden collapse it had become a semiliquid heap of black and horrible putrescence which stained the dais and poisoned the air. At the same time Scanlan and I dashed forward onto the platform, for Dr. Maracot, with a deep groan, his powers exhausted, had fallen forward in helpless collapse. "We have won! We have won!" he muttered, and an instant later his senses had left him and he lay half-dead upon the floor.

Thus it was the Atlantean Colony was saved from the most horrible danger that could threaten it, and that an evil presence was banished forever from the world. It was not for some days that Dr. Maracot could tell his story, and when he did it was of such a character that if we had not seen the results we should have put it down as the delirium of his illness. I may say that his power had left him with the occasion which had called it forth, and that he was now the same quiet, gentle man of science whom we had known.

"That it should have happened to me!" he cried. "To me, a materialist, a man so immersed in matter that the invisible did not exist in my philosophy. The theories of a whole lifetime have crumbled about my ears."

"I guess we have all been to school again," said

Scanlan. "If ever I get back to the little home town, I shall have something to tell the boys."

"The less you tell them the better, unless you want to get the name of being the greatest liar that ever came out of America," said I. "Would you or I have believed it all if someone else had told us?"

"Maybe not. But say, Doc, you had the dope right enough. That great black stiff got his ten and out as neat as ever I saw. There was no comeback there. You clean pushed him off the map. I don't know on what other map he has found his location, but it is no place for Bill Scanlan anyhow."

"I will tell you exactly what occurred," said the Doctor. "You will remember that I left you and retired into my study. I had little hope in my heart, but I had read a good deal at different times about black magic and occult arts. I was aware that white can always dominate black if it can but reach the same plane. He was on a much stronger—I will not say higher—plane than we. That was the fatal fact.

"I saw no way of getting over it. I flung myself down on the settee and I prayed—yes, I, the hardened materialist, prayed -for help. When one is at the very end of all human power, what can one do save to stretch appealing hands into the mists which gird us round? I prayed—and my prayer was most wonderfully answered.

"I was suddenly aware of the fact that I was not alone in the room. There stood before me a tall figure, as swarthy as the evil presence whom we fought, but with a kindly, bearded face which shone with benevolence and love. The sense of power which he conveyed was not less than the other, but it was the power of good, the power within the influence of which evil would shred away as the mists do before the sun. He looked at me with kindly eyes, and I sat, too amazed to speak, staring up at him. Something within me, some inspiration or intuition, told me that this was the spirit of that great and wise Atlantean who had fought the evil while he lived, and who, when he could not prevent the destruction of his country, took such steps as would ensure that the more worthy should survive even though they should be sunk to the depths of the ocean. This wondrous being was now interposing to prevent the ruin of his work and the destruction of his children. With a sudden gush of hope I realized all this as clearly as if he had said it. Then, still smiling, he advanced, and he laid his two hands upon my head. It was his own virtue and strength, no doubt, which he was transferring to me. I felt it coursing like fire down my veins. Nothing in the world seemed impossible at that moment. I had the will and the might to do miracles. Then at that moment I heard the bell clang out, which told me that the crisis had come. As I rose from the couch the spirit, smiling his encouragement, vanished before me. Then I joined you, and the rest you know."

"Well, sir," said I, "I think you have made your reputation. If you care to set up as a god down here, I expect you would find no difficulty."

"You got away with it better than I did, Doc," said Scanlan in a rueful voice. "How is it this guy didn't know what you were doing? He was quick enough on to me when I laid hand on a gun. And yet you had him guessing."

"I suppose that you were on the plane of matter, and that, for the moment, we were upon that of spirit," said the Doctor thoughtfully. "Such things teach one humility. It is only when you touch the higher that you realize how low we may be among the possibilities of creation. I have had my lesson. May my future life show that I have learned it."

So this was the end of our supreme experience. It was but a little time later that we conceived the idea of sending news of ourselves to the surface, and that later, by means of vitrine balls filled with levigen, we ascended ourselves to be met in the manner already narrated. Dr. Maracot actually talks of going back. There is some point of Ichthyology upon which he wants more precise information. But Scanlan has, I hear, married his wren in Philadelphia, and has been promoted as works manager of Merribank's, so he seeks no further adventure, while I—well, the deep sea has given me a precious pearl, and I ask for no more.